Damned if I don't

ALSO BY SCARLETT KNOX

Heaven and Hell Chronicles
Damned if I do
Damned if I don't
Damned if I know

the Vampires of Knightsbridge
Monster of Fate

AS E.J. KNOX

Sinners of Saint Benedicts

Gods & Angels

Princes & Wolves

Men & Monsters

Rivermont Royals
Reign
Rival

Rivermont Royals Reveals
Obsess
Infatuate

Little Nymph
Little Nymph
Little Secret

Immortals of Lionswood Academy
Pawn takes Knight
Knight take Bishop

<u>**AS PIPPA LANGHORN**</u>
Love to Hate You
Heat of the Moment

<u>**AS ELIZABETH STEVENS**</u>
the Trouble with Hate is…
Being Not Good
Popped
the Art of Breaking Up

Accidentally Perfect Books
Accidentally Perfect
Perfectly Accidental

Royal Misadventures
Now Presenting
Lady in Training
Three of a Kind
Some Proposal
Royally Unprepared
Royals in Dating

AVAILABLE ON WATTPAD
Austen Reimagined
Pride
Prejudice

the Danu Cycle
Gryffynhall
Elfhaven

the Damned Trilogy: Book 2

Damned if I don't

ELIZABETH STEVENS WRITING AS
SCARLETT KNOX

Kinky Siren, an imprint of Sleeping Dragon Books

Damned if I don't
by Scarlett Knox

Print ISBN: **978-1925928235**
Digital ISBN: 978-1925928228

Cover art by: Izzie Duffield

Copyright 2020 Elizabeth Stevens

Worldwide Electronic & Digital Rights
Worldwide English Language Print Rights

All rights reserved. No part of this book may be reproduced, scanned or distributed in any form, including digital and electronic or mechanical, including photocopying, recording, or by any information storage and retrieval system, without the prior written consent of the Publisher, except for brief quotes for use in reviews. This book is a work of fiction. Characters, names, places and incidents either are the product of the author's imagination or are used fictitiously, and any resemblance to any actual persons, living or dead, events, or locales is entirely coincidental.

For Stephanie from LA,
For reading all my books and liking them so much I hear
about it on the other side of the world.
You made my day ☺

Contents

One: Wren.. 1
Two: Drake 14
Three: Wren 27
Four: Drake 34
Five: Wren 45
Six: Drake 54
Seven: Wren 63
Eight: Drake..................................... 70
Nine: Wren..................................... 78
Ten: Drake 91
Eleven: Wren..................................... 97
Twelve: Drake 105
Thirteen: Wren 111
Fourteen: Drake..................................... 119
Fifteen: Wren 126
Sixteen: Drake 135
Seventeen: Wren 145
Eighteen: Drake 151
Nineteen: Wren 157
Twenty: Drake..................................... 165
Twenty-One: Wren 174
Damned if I don't..................................... 183
Thanks..................................... 184
My Books..................................... 185
About the Author 186

Wren

To say being married to the son of Lucifer required an adjustment period would be an understatement. And, besides Harmony, my parents were probably the ones who were taking it the best.

"Does the tablecloth look too formal?" Mum asked as I walked into the dining room.

I focussed my eyes on her to see her smoothing over the tablecloth and glaring at it like it had betrayed her.

"For most meetings of the in-laws, ma'am, perhaps," Truman answered her from his perch standing on one of the dining chairs. "But I assure you that his lordship won't have any complaints."

"He likes it formal?"

Truman nodded. "Yes, ma'am. He…enjoys any chance to dress up."

"He doesn't need it to be formal for that," I commented dryly.

"Ma'am." Truman bowed to me and I nodded back in greeting.

Mum looked at me with a smile. "Do you think Gran's blue set or the white and gold?"

I shrugged. "I don't think it will matter."

"Okay. But if you were going to be helpful and work with me to get ready to meet your father-in-law, which one would you suggest?" her tone was chastising, but her smile was as cheeky as it ever got.

"Mum, I honestly have no idea," I said, failing to hide my own smile.

"And what are you going to do when you and Drake have dinner parties?" she asked, folding her arms. "You'd best just stick with the one dinner setting. Hopefully you're more helpful in picking it out for Gran than you are right now." I didn't say anything and she mistook my silence for there being another option. "Although, I suppose you *will* have Truman and the boys to help you."

But I wasn't thinking about how cool it was that I'd have beings to set up and organise any party I hosted from now on. I wasn't wistfully thinking about what sort of pattern I wanted on my china, the traditional wedding gift from Gran. I wasn't even wondering where the other two boys were or what on Earth they might be getting up to. I was having a sudden shiver of cold feet.

What the Heaven had I been thinking, literally tramping through Hell to demand to be with Drake? I was far too young for this. I wasn't ready. Quite obviously demonstrated by the fact I couldn't muster up a single shred of maturity to help Mum choose which dinner set to use for dinner with my father-in-law.

"True, ma'am," Truman offered. "If Mistress Serenity so wishes, she will have the whole of Hell at her beck and call for party hosting."

"Oh, well. It's quite nice for some. Isn't it?" Mum chuckled to him.

"There are some perks to the damned, ma'am."

"Do these perks extend to in-laws?" Mum asked.

Truman inclined his head. "I'm sure it would be possible to arrange, ma'am."

"Oh. That *is* quite nice."

There was silence. I was still panicking. But I thought I was hiding it well.

"Wren?" Mum asked.

I blinked and huffed a ridiculously nervous laugh. "Yes?"

She frowned. "You okay?"

I nodded. "Fine," I squeaked. I cleared my throat and tried again. "Fine. Fine. Why?"

"You just…spaced out for a while." Mum paused as though she could determine my 'okayness' just by looking at me. Obviously, she decided it was not something to push hours before Lucifer arrived. "If you're not going to be a help with the dinner set, can you check the oven please?"

I nodded. "Sure."

Thankful to have a reason to at least somewhat satisfy my urge to run, I hurried to the kitchen.

"What are you doing?" I muttered to myself angrily.

I knew, without a doubt, I wasn't backing out of this now. Drake was mine as I was his for eternity. I hadn't bothered asking – which seemed a mistake in hindsight – but I doubted if there was any way to break that. I was pretty sure the whole 'til death us do part' bit didn't count when one of you was immortal and resided in the afterlife.

Not that I actually wanted to back out, even if it was possible.

A girl was allowed a small freak out now and then, wasn't she? I mean, I was allowed to panic about whether I'd rushed into being married before I even finished school. That was just sensible, wasn't it?

My problem was that sensible had no place in my relationship with Drake. Everything about being with him worked differently than any human relationship would have. Time meant nothing to him, not the way it did to me. And, being with him, I could forget what my upbringing had instilled in me about timeframes and when was appropriate to do things. It all felt natural and normal and right. But without him, as I was just then, my human life came rushing back in and I started trying to second-guess everything.

After a few days together post-formalisation of our relationship, I came back to Earth to finish school. Sure, I could have put it off for longer, could have stayed with him for an immeasurable amount of time and still made it back in time for my exams. I probably could have just had Drake make it so I passed my exams however I wanted. But I'd just wanted to put that phase of my life behind me and it felt like a good ritual in which to do it. Plus, I wanted the accomplishment (or failure) to be entirely my own.

Harmony took full advantage of my marriage twice. We went to Hell to get some cramming in, essentially locking Drake out of our room so we could concentrate. Harmony had no problem telling me he was a distracting presence, and not just because he was bloody sexy but also our apparent sexual tension was hotter than Hell, literally. I had no problem with her telling me any of this; I both agreed with her and had no concerns she was even entertaining the notion of wanting him for herself.

So, Drake and I basically hadn't seen each other at all since I'd left Hell after those few glorious days. I'd lived five weeks. He must have lived years.

I'd loved having time with my family and friends, but I was terrified that everything would have changed in that time. I was terrified that Drake had got over the 'despondent missing me' stage to the 'used to my absence' phase, through the 'was I actually married?' portion, and wouldn't want me anymore.

It was a stark reminder of the fact there were two different sides to my life.

On one hand, I was the wife of Lucifer's son. I was fearless and strong and knew exactly what I wanted. I'd literally walked through Hell with nothing but three devilbums and my love for Drake.

On the other, I was just another human in the world. Insignificant in the grand scheme, but still managing to do it all wrong anyway. I worried and didn't know what I wanted and didn't know how I'd even go about making everything work together if I did know what I wanted.

It was a mess and one I would be happy to be rid of as soon as Drake and Lucifer arrived later that night. Whether my husband still wanted me or not, at least I'd be able to put this restless uncertainty to…well, rest.

"How's it looking, ma'am?"

I turned to smile at Truman. He'd been a huge help to Mum, happy to assist with cooking and housework and gardening. He seemed totally in his element and I didn't think I'd ever seen him more content – to say Truman was happy might have been a gross overstatement.

"I…think it's okay?" I said uncertainly.

Truman trotted over to the oven and peered in. "And how are you, ma'am?" he asked nonchalantly.

I tucked a piece of hair behind my ear and nodded. "Good. Good. Fine."

"Are you sure, ma'am?"

I cleared my throat and asked the question I'd been putting off. "You would have – like – heard…if they weren't coming tonight, right?" I asked quickly, like ripping off a band-aid.

"Of course, ma'am. Messenger demon popped up this morning to confirm they were well on their way."

I breathed a shaky sigh of semi-relief. I'd fully believe it when I saw him, but that was going to have to be enough for now. As though he could read my mind – although he'd assured me devilbums didn't have that power – Truman turned and clasped his claws in front of him.

"Might I suggest a nice bath and a relax, ma'am?" he said. "Give you a pamper and you'll be right as rain for tonight."

I found myself smiling at him. "Thank you, Truman. That sounds…" I looked around. "You don't need any help with anything?"

Truman's red leathery face contorted into the devilbum equivalent of the eyebrow raise. "I think you'd be more useful relaxing, ma'am."

I often appreciated his sassy straight-laced nature. Just then, I was on the fence about it, but only because it wasn't usually aimed at me. "I'm choosing to take that positively."

"A sound choice, ma'am."

"Kyle helping," he cooed as he hurried through the kitchen and into the dining room.

He was carrying a chair that was about two times bigger than him, dressed in his little apron. Ignacio appeared, much slower paced, carrying another chair. He spared me a nod on the way by.

"What is Mum doing?" I asked.

"Your father is polishing the furniture. Your mother felt it prudent to do as much of it in the garage as possible."

I looked at him and he, again, seemed able to read my mind.

He nodded. "I offered, but she said we were doing this the human way. It was apparently also a good way to keep your father occupied and not messing up the house."

That made sense. I nodded. "Right. Of course."

Mum and Dad had taken the day off work – Tilly was finished uni for the year but told in no uncertain circumstances that she should stay out of the house or in her room – in order to get everything finalised for Lucifer's arrival. My exams had finished earlier that week, so all I had stretching out in front of me was the whole rest of my life.

As though that wasn't thoroughly terrifying and incredibly exciting all at the same time.

As Kyle came trotting back into the room, Truman caught him.

"Kyle, can you assist Mistress Serenity this afternoon?"

Kyle looked between us, his bat ears flopping as his head moved. "Yup. Kyle help how?"

"Mistress Serenity is going to take a nice long bath and relax in preparation for tonight. I need you to take care of her and make sure she's relaxing properly."

Kyle spun around with his arms in the air. "Yes! Kyle do that."

He grabbed my hand and started pulling me towards the stairs.

"Relaxing, Kyle. Mistress Serenity needs to relax!" Truman called as Kyle and I headed upstairs.

"Yep. Yep. Yep!" Kyle called back.

Kyle got me into the bath, relaxingly warm but not too hot for the weather, and started waiting on me hand and foot. He ferried drinks in and out, snacks, books and magazines. I didn't want or need all of it, but I was also loath to wipe the big goofy smile off his face. The little guy wasn't usually super useful, and I knew he enjoyed the times he felt he was.

It wasn't at all weird being naked in front of them anymore. None of them cared about what I looked like in any state of dress or undress. It had freaked Tilly out one time when Truman had wandered into the bathroom when she was in there once. But, since, the whole family had sort of just got used to them doing their thing regardless of what was going on.

Ignacio was still helping Dad out with things. It had taken a while, but we had taught him not to just attack anything and everything that gave us the slightest annoyance. Now, he looked at things for a while in order to deduce their actual danger factor before he attacked it teeth-first.

I was replying to a message from Harmony when I felt I was being watched. I looked out the corner of my eyes and found Kyle watching me. His claws were gripping the side of the bath and all I could see were his eyes, horns, and ears, but I knew he wore a wide smile. I had an idea of what he was thinking about.

"Yes, Kyle?" I asked, trying not to laugh at him.

"Harmony coming tonight?" he asked sheepishly.

I shook my head. "Sorry, buddy. Not tonight."

His ears deflated and his eyes went all forlorn. "Oh."

I rubbed his head. "But we might see her tomorrow?"

"Serenity see Drake tomorrow."

I nodded and hoped I hadn't given away the way my heart lurched. "I can do both, can't I?"

There was this mischievous look in his eyes now. "Serenity and Drake will want alone time. Kyle could see Harmony."

I chuckled. "Okay. How about I see what she's doing and if she says it's okay you can go and see her for a little bit while Drake and I are…" I didn't need to finish that sentence. We both knew what Drake and I would be up to for Kyle to be not needed.

"Okay!" Kyle said happily.

As I was sending a message to Harmony about it, Truman wandered in.

"Ma'am, might I suggest it time to get dressed?" he asked.

I looked at him, then checked the time on my phone. "Shit, it's later than I thought."

"Still plenty of time, ma'am."

"I need to wash my hair!" I cried, annoyed I hadn't been keeping a proper eye on the time.

"Ma'am," Truman chided.

I looked at him and sighed. "All right. Just this once."

He gave what passed for a smile from him and nodded. "Wonderful."

I jumped out of the bath and Kyle handed me a towel, exaggeratedly not looking at me until I was covered in the weird little way he had – no one cared about my nakedness, but he liked to go through the motions of pretending we did.

Truman trotted ahead into my room and Kyle and I followed.

"All right," I said, resignedly. "Do your worst."

Truman nodded and looked me over. There was the briefest flash of flames licking my body and then I was styled and dressed. I'd avoided making use of the boys' powers as much as possible – there was something nice about doing all those things myself, a sense of accomplishment – but I wasn't going to pass them up when it meant I'd be late otherwise.

I hurried downstairs and into the dining room. It looked amazing. Flowers in full bloom stood in vases around the room. The candelabras were polished and the candles flickering merrily. The table was set like I'd just walked onto the set of Downton Abbey. Plates and cutlery and glasses all sat perfectly aligned.

"Mum, this looks amazing," I told her.

She looked up from the knife she was rearranging. "Oh, thank you, darling. Feeling better?"

I nodded. "I think so."

Now it was so close, I actually thought I felt worse. My heart fluttered erratically and it was like I'd forgotten how to breathe properly. Only exacerbated when the doorbell rang and I nearly jumped out of my skin.

"They're here," Mum said happily.

I nodded again.

"Well, aren't you going to let them in? You must be dying to see him."

"Oh. Yes!"

I hurried to the door and forced myself to take a deep breath.

Finally, I pulled the door open and there he was.

He looked the same as always. Youthful, but ageless. Toned. Angry. That aura of danger. And the heavily intense gaze that didn't leave me. He wore a simple shirt and jeans, same as usual. But just then nothing had ever looked better to me.

2

Drake

It had been too holy long. I was just about out of my mind for having been without her for so long. Fucking years had passed for me while five weeks had passed for her. I'd spent my time as only a prince of Hell could.

Souls to torture.

Cadriel to beat to a fucking pulp.

Getting beaten to a fucking pulp.

Dinners and shows with my father.

Month after month without even the devilbums for company.

And feeling like I'd lost a part of myself the whole saved time. It was made worse knowing she was just out of reach and that I'd see her again…only after an agonising wait.

When my mum had died, that was it. She was gone. I had no choice but to move on once the distractions weren't so shiny.

But I would never move on from Wren. She was a part of me I hadn't known I was missing. She literally had my soul now and that wasn't something I could undo. Even death couldn't sever our bond – Thane had tried it once to no effect, but that's another story.

Being without her had been a torture even my father couldn't have devised. And the souls paid the price for it dearly. Dad had created a room in which whoever went in there felt it all, everything I was feeling. That was it. That was the torture. My parting from my wife.

I shrugged it off and tried to play it cool, but even Cadriel could tell how bad it was. He never said anything. It was all in the fact he didn't say anything. If Cadriel had anything going for him, it was that he could read a soul like an open book. He knew how to push your buttons, and he knew *when* to push your buttons. It had got him in trouble with more than a few souls in his time.

But I was moments away from seeing her now and I felt like Kyle on Samhain. I had to force myself not to bounce on my toes in anticipation.

I'd made Dad wait outside the front door like a normal person. He hadn't even argued, deciding it was fun to play human for a while. I even let him ring the doorbell.

There was a pause in which I thought being damned was the worst of my problems.

What if she'd changed her mind? What if being back in the human world this long had made her reconsider our marriage? What if she wanted to stay?

After what felt like forever – and, remember, I'd lived it so I'd know – the door opened and there she was.

I felt like I'd only just remembered how to breathe again. I felt like my heart had never really beaten until now. My entire world stood before me locked away in the body of an unbearably small and fragile human being. But I didn't know how not to adore her. I didn't want to know.

"Hi," she said, smiling softly as she tucked a piece of hair behind her ear.

"Serenity, darling," Dad said warmly as he stepped forward and hugged her.

"Oh, hi," she laughed as she hugged him back, but her eyes didn't leave mine.

There were so many things I wanted to do to her. Very few of them were acceptable in front of other beings, and the rest weren't something I'd be caught mortal doing in front of anyone else.

Dad finally let my wife go.

"Um, please come in. We're through here," Wren said, pointing to her left.

Dad helped himself in, peering around doorways and tiptoeing all excitedly like it was Uncle Jesus' 'birthday' and he wanted to try to catch old Nick in the act.

But my wife was standing in front of me and we had a modicum of privacy.

"Hey, neighbour," I said and her lips blossomed into a smile.

"Hey."

I took two steps towards her, my heart beating unrestrained in my chest. My hand just reached out for hers. I was millimetres from touching her. I was inches from tasting her. But I was forced to stumble backwards as Kyle flung himself onto my leg.

"Drake!" he cried happily. "Kyle missed Drake."

"Good to see you too, Kyle." I looked at Wren as I patted his head.

She bit her lip to stop herself from laughing at me. Grandad, how I'd missed her. I'd always thought that the whole 'absence makes the heart grow fonder thing was bullshit'. In my experience, the burning ache of absence faded to little more than fragments of memory and fostered apathy. But I was definitely feeling fonder for my wife than I was sure I had when she'd left.

"Wren!" her mum called and she looked at me apologetically.

"Coming."

"Not yet," I said softly and she grinned knowingly.

She held her hand out for Kyle, who took it unhesitatingly, and led us into the dining room. I barely had time to wonder what they'd been up to, what routines they'd fallen into without me, when I had to put my game face on. I wasn't the sort to play at nice and polite, but this was my wife's family. I wanted them to not hate me and talk her out of staying with me.

"Sorry," Wren said as we walked in to see our parents and her sister hovering around. "So…Lucifer, these are my parents, Steph and Brian Shaw, and my sister, Tilly. Guys, this is Lucifer Morningstar…" Wren looked at him like she wasn't sure if that had been the right introduction, but he only grinned at her.

"Mr and Mrs Shaw, it is a pleasure," Dad said, bowing. The guy would have looked insincere if you didn't know him; dude wasn't about to do anything to jeopardise his chance to plan a party and on Earth no less.

"Oh, please," Steph tittered as Dad took her hand. "Call me Steph."

"Steph, then," Dad said, placing a kiss on her, then extending a hand to Wren's dad with a prim nod. "Brian."

"Lucifer."

For a mortal man being faced with the literal devil, Brian was doing a stand-up job of keeping his cool. But then, he'd lived with Ignacio for about two months. Compared to Ignacio, my father – like this – would seem tame.

"And, Tilly?" Dad asked, looking around.

Tilly nodded and shuffled forward. Apparently, living with the boys had given her a different expectation of my father than Brian.

"Short for Matilda," she said.

"*Enchanté*." Dad smirked and kissed her hand.

She giggled. "Oh. Thank you." Aside from her eyes constantly shifting to me, she seemed quite happy to just watch everything with those wide eyes and stay as inconspicuous as possible. It was a sight different than the last time I'd seen her.

"So, I brought Alexander's favourite wine!" Dad said cheerfully, always one to hate silence, as he held it up and I rolled my eyes.

"Oh…" Brian said. "Who's Alexander?"

"Judging by that jug, the Great," Steph laughed. She totally meant it as a joke.

Dad obviously didn't notice or chose not to notice. "See," he said to me. "Someone appreciates these things."

"Oh," Steph said. "Was that…? Did you *actually* mean Alexander the Great?"

Dad nodded with a proud smile. "Of course."

"My father thinks it makes him look good."

Dad practically stamped his foot at me. "I am the Lord of Hell. It has perks. Let me show off my perks!"

"I keep telling you, it only works when they know who he is."

"Steph knows who he is!"

"That's… Uh, that was very nice of you," Steph said quickly, obviously trying to abort any celestial family fight that might have been about to happen in her dining room. "It's very apprecia–"

Her words ended on a yelp, but it wasn't quite as loud or high-pitched as my father's shriek as the being appeared right next to him.

"The perimeter is clear," he droned, his deep black wings folding back to nothing.

"I.. Oh…" Brian said, nodding like it made sense to him.

"How many times have I told you not to do that!" Dad snapped, trying to regain his composure.

Thank Grandad he didn't drop Alexander's favourite wine.

Steph and Brian were doing their best to act like it was common occurrence for beings to just appear in their dining room. Tilly seemed a little pre-occupied with waiting to see if anything more remarkable than disappearing wings was going to occur. Wren, with Kyle attached to her leg, was just taking it all in her stride. Her confusion stemmed more from her not recognising the angel rather than surprise an angel had materialised in her parents' dining room.

"Shaws, allow me to introduce Samyeza. He's going to be…" I cleared my throat, sharing a glare with the great big angel. "He'll be my guard while I'm on Earth."

There were a lot of contentious issues about that statement. Had I been willing to believe I needed a guard, I didn't see why it couldn't have at least been Cadriel. Samyeza and I had had a rather epic battle over the whole issue and I'd lost. Badly. It had been my most embarrassing and convincing loss to date, and that includes the time I'd slept with Samael's wife and he'd shown me just what he thought of that.

"Guard?" Steph asked, looking between us in motherly concern. "Are you in danger, dear?"

"Every day of his existence," Dad said, for all the world talking about how nice the weather was. "My father's *beloved* sons aren't too fond of mine." He helped himself to sitting at the dining table and everyone else – but Samyeza – followed suit, Kyle climbing into Wren's lap to be involved. "And particularly so when they've *fallen* out of His favour." He chuckled proudly.

I held in the sigh at his attempt at a joke. "The Fallen are trying desperately to get back into Grandad's good books by killing all Nephilim," I explained.

"Half angel, half human." Dad started pouring wine as he took over. "And since Samyeza was the one who first suggested the angels and the humans engage in a little…hanky panky, he feels honour-bound to protect them."

Samyeza, still standing in the room like some poorly placed marble statue, managed to keep his expression relatively neutral. But it wasn't like the guy looked approachable on any given day. Not while he was working or hanging out with the damned anyway.

"Oh, that's nice," Steph said. "Are there…many Nephilim, then? For you to keep an eye on." She looked at Samyeza, but he wasn't going to respond.

"Hundreds," I answered.

"Goodness. How does…Samyeza manage to look after them all?"

"Oh, he doesn't," Dad said, waving his hand at her. "That's the job of the Nephilim Protection Squad."

"There's a…?" Wren asked.

Kyle shook his head wildly as I told her, "That's what my father calls them."

"What? It's a good name. There's a bunch of Grigori, like a squad you might say. They protect Nephilim. It works. Anyway, Samyeza leads all Grigori. And he's doing this little favour for me in looking after Drake while he's…topside, shall we say."

Favour was a bit of a stretch. Samyeza had insisted only he would be good enough to protect me. One of my ribs was still healing because of the…strength of his insistence.

I caught Wren's eyes and I could see she was hiding the extent of her worry.

We'd had very few conversations about just what kind of idea it was to have me on Earth. I'd downplayed the potential danger I would be in if Azazel's men found out I was here.

There were only two possibilities when it came to me. Either Azazel would decide that trying to kill Lucifer's son was suicide, or killing me would be exactly the ticket to getting back in Grandad's good books. There was a fuck tonne of protocol Azazel would have to follow if he did decide to try to kill me. Not in the least that humanity was supposed to be kept out of the loop of our existence on the whole.

But now wasn't really the time to go into it all, and Dad seemed to realise that.

"But that's all terribly boring." He clapped his hands together. "I want to talk about the wedding!"

So, of course, we talked about the wedding. Most of it was parental and sibling input – wasn't I glad I didn't know most of my siblings and cousins – while Wren and I sat across the table from each other. I lived with literal flames and I'd never been hotter than I was under her green gaze just then.

Truman and the boys started to ferry the first lot of food and drink in.

Truman gave me a short head incline and a, "Master."

Ignacio gave me what counted as a smile in his short list of facial expressions and a, "Boss."

Kyle beamed from ear to ear and told me, "Kyle good at helping."

"Yes, you are," Steph said. "But let me help, boys."

"Nonsense, ma'am," Truman said. "You've done plenty. Sit and enjoy yourself."

Steph smiled happily and accepted Dad's offer of more wine.

"So, have we chosen the dress yet?" Dad asked as he started eating. "Oh, Steph. This is lovely."

"Oh, thank you," she chuckled.

I got through the first course by trying not to look at Wren. But it was difficult. Most of Dad's conversation was trying to pull her into the wedding planning. And every time I heard her voice, I had to look at her. And I knew she knew what I'd rather be doing.

When the plates were empty, she started collecting them.

"Ma'am, let us," Truman said.

"No!" she said loudly. "No. I'll help."

"Let me," I said, standing and starting to collect plates as well.

As we both walked out, I heard Dad say none too quietly, "Well, those two definitely want some private time."

I didn't care the whole table now probably knew what I wanted to do to her. All that mattered was I got to touch her.

We both practically threw our piles of plates on the bench and turned to each other.

"I missed you," she said.

I smirked. "I missed you."

She wrapped her arms around my neck and I pulled her close to me.

"How much did you miss me?" she asked.

"More than I can show you right now."

"Why don't you give me a little taste?" She leant up to me.

Our lips were about to touch when Dad walked in.

"I was told the wine was… Oh!" he chuckled. "Silly me. Getting in the way."

Wren pulled away from me and smiled. "Not at all. What were you after?"

"Wine. Your delightful mother said the fridge…?"

I took a deep breath and tried to keep my cool. I didn't know if there was an equivalent for cock blocking for a simple kiss, but my father was quite clearly a master at every kind of blocking known to creation.

I watched Wren help him find whatever he was looking for and lead him back into the dining room.

"Hard night, sir?" Truman asked me.

I glared at him. "You have no idea."

"Oh, I don't know, sir. I think I have quite a good idea."

I looked at him in question. His eyes darted down for a second and I followed his glance.

"Right. Thank you. Back to work," I muttered.

I rearranged the bulge in my jeans and headed back to dinner with the in-laws.

Wren

It had taken forever, but Drake and I finally had a moment to ourselves. The cheese and fruit had been eaten, Lucifer had resorted to conjuring alcohol because they'd drunk it all, and Mum, Dad, he and Tilly were all dancing around in the living room.

Drake took my hand and pulled me out of the room while no one else was watching.

I laughed as I looked back to see Tilly dancing with Kyle. But I was soon far too distracted.

Drake pressed me against the wall in the hallway. One arm leant on the wall behind me. One hand went to my hip to keep me close to his body. And his forehead dropped to mine. His eyes went from blue to bright red as I looked into them. I got a flutter in my chest that spread through my body and tingled in my stomach.

"And just what are you planning?" I asked him cheekily.

There was a faint hint of a smile in his eyes that I knew would be little more than a wry half-smirk at his lips. "On giving you more than just a taste of how much I missed you."

I wrapped my arms around his neck and held him close. "I worried you'd be over me."

The look in his eyes told me how ridiculous he thought I sounded. "Over you?" he said softly and his tone mirrored his eyes. His nose nudged mine gently. "You could spend another twelve years without me and I wouldn't be over you. You could end up with Grandad for eternity and I wouldn't be over you. I have never been more certain about anything than I am about you, Serenity. You were born to be my wife, and I born to be your husband."

I couldn't find words to say. I was too full of emotions and happiness and just everything that was him and me and us that nothing would come. So, I kissed him and hoped actions really did speak louder than words.

And I was pretty sure they did.

Our kiss didn't take long to go from the kind of deep, emotional passion to hands seeking the best way to remove clothing quickly.

Someone laughed in the dining room, reminding me we weren't as alone as I'd like. So, I grabbed his hand and pulled him up to my room.

Drake pushed the door closed – my body between it and him – and picked me up to press me into it. I felt him hard between my legs and felt just how much I'd missed him in more ways than one.

We'd barely left our room before I'd come back to finish school. And without the fear of separation holding us back, we didn't hesitate to explore each other's bodies all over. Poor Kyle had been terribly put out that we kept sending him out of the room. But our desire seemed insatiable and, without worrying about taking things too far, we'd had sex when we wanted how we wanted.

I'd thought that maybe it would be different after being apart. But his kiss was just as heated. His cock was just as hard. His hands on me were just as possessive and demanding. He still sent the same flash of burning need through me. A need I just knew he reciprocated.

"We shouldn't be gone too long," I panted as his kiss moved down my neck.

"Is that what you really want?" he asked.

I sighed. "Probably not," I admitted as he pressed his erection into me tantalisingly.

"But you feel obligated?"

I nodded vaguely. "That."

His hand skimmed up the underside of my leg towards my panty line. I bit my lip as he nipped my neck softly.

"So, you want me to be quick?" he asked slowly, his voice deep and growly.

My hand fisted in his hair as we rubbed together and I nodded. "I guess so."

He dropped me to the floor and spun me around with one movement, pulling my arse into his hardness. He leant his chest to my back and caught my earlobe in his mouth.

"I promise nothing," he said roughly.

My undies were gone and he ran his hand over my arse appreciatively. He pulled my body to his again, massaging my breast with one hand as the other rested low on my abdomen.

"How much did you miss me?" he rasped.

My head leant back on his chest as the hand on my abdomen slid further down.

"More than I knew was possible," I told him. I sucked in a needy breath as his fingers trailed over my clit.

"What did you miss?"

"Everything."

"Tell me."

"I missed the way you looked at me."

"How do I look at you?" he demanded as he rubbed over my clit more purposefully.

I breathed deeply. "Like you want me. Like you love me."

His hand left my breast and he started undoing his jeans. "How does that make you feel?"

"Powerful," I gasped wantonly as he thrust into me.

He leant his hand on the door, his body encasing mine, as his other teased me and he thrust into me slowly and steadily.

"You're a goddess, Wren," he told me fiercely. "I would walk into Heaven for you. I've never known torture like being without you. I wanted to keep you safe, let you live a full life, but I was selfish. I need you. Only you."

He was thrusting faster, harder, with every sentence.

Passion swirled around us and I'd never felt as truly wanted like that in my life. It was sexy. It was heart-warming. Emotion and feeling were building inside me, his words and his body working me expertly.

It wasn't just lust, it was romance. Maybe not the kind Disney had told me about, but it was mine and that made it oh so perfect.

"Drake," I moaned, feeling tingles spread through my body. "I need you."

In one swift move, he'd pulled out, flipped me around and had me against the door. I didn't even have time to bemoan his withdrawal before he was inside me again.

"I love you," I told him, wishing there was some way to really convey just how deeply I felt for him. Three little words just didn't seem to cut it.

"Oh, Wren," he groaned.

He kissed me hard and we moved together as one. Frenetic and desperate, we came hard together. There was nothing gentle in our reunion. But he was the heir to Hell. If I'd wanted gentle, I would have stayed on Earth.

We didn't make it back downstairs all night and I didn't care if our family knew why.

When I woke the next morning in Drake's arms, I almost felt like I was still dreaming. I stretched, my eyes scrunching as I did. I felt warm and gooey inside and not like getting up at all.

"Then don't," Drake mumbled, his nose nuzzling under my ear.

I smiled. "Get out of my head."

"I didn't mean to," he said softly in that gravelly morning voice I loved so much.

I opened my eyes and rolled to look at him. "How does it happen?"

He shrugged a little and pulled me to him, my leg going over his side. "I can turn it on and off. I can listen in to specific people or everyone. Sometimes," his nose nudged mine, "I wonder what you're thinking when you wake up and it happens by accident."

"Well isn't it good my subconscious didn't choose to give me a sex dream about someone else last night?" I teased.

The corner of his lip tipped up and his eyes shone bright red as they looked into mine, igniting a very metaphorical fire in me. And it wasn't all just about sex. "Do you have sex dreams about other beings often?"

I shook my head with a wry smile. "No. I can't remember the last time it wasn't you."

He pushed me against the bed, rolling over me. "Good." His knee slid up, parting my legs slightly. "You let me know if that changes. I will be more than happy to wipe all memory of it from your head."

We stared into each other's eyes for the space of a heartbeat.

After the night before, I felt used in the best kind of way. But I still wanted him. I felt like I'd never get enough of him.

He might not have actually outright said he loved me, but he didn't have to. He said it in other ways. Other words. The look in his eyes as they bored into mine, whether they were blue or red. It was in the way he touched me, sure and firm but also like I was precious.

In his arms, it felt right. I had no doubts, no worries. Just a certainty that, whatever happened, we'd face it together and we'd triumph every time.

Drake

I'd have been an idiot to not see the split-second hesitation in her now and then. I tried so hard to respect her privacy and it saved near killed me to stay out of her head except by accident.

So, despite it making me feel physically sick, I asked her what was wrong when I was about to succumb to the wrong kind of temptation. She'd looked at me with this winning smile, all soft and thoughtful as she searched my eyes.

"Sometimes I have to remind myself I'm not dreaming," she said. "I worry I'm going to wake up and realise I still have five weeks of not seeing you or you'll never turn up."

I pulled her close. "I will always turn up."

"I know."

I heard the certainty in her voice and all my mild panic dissolved. She wasn't second-guessing us. If anything, she was, like me, worried it might all come to an end. Or worse, that it had never happened in the first place. I never wanted to let her go for fear either would prove real. But I'd had to drag myself out of her bed and out of her arms at some point because she wasn't the only one with responsibilities.

Just because I was on Earth, didn't mean I was to be allowed to go soft. So, Cadriel met me at the address my father had given me for his, quote, "Crash pad."

"Ahoy," Dad answered the gate intercom.

"This is what you're calling a crash pad?" I asked as Kyle said, "Ahoy," back.

"Drake! Come in. Come in!" The line disconnected.

"It's a fucking McMansion," I muttered as we waited for the gates to open.

I kicked the bike into gear and edged up the ridiculously long and winding driveway. Wren had initially been hesitant to let me drive a motorcycle. However, once I'd let Ignacio crash it into me with no (read: limited) adverse effects, she merely informed me that she wouldn't be caught dead on it. Deciding I quite liked her alive, I acceded to her wishes and didn't suggest she get on it, even for the sake of some sexual innuendo.

As I pulled up to the front door, Cadriel landed in front of me.

"How's Hell coping without their melodramatic leader?" I asked the Grigori as I got off the bike and pulled off my helmet.

"Do you really want to know?" he asked me as he folded his wings back into non-existence.

I looked at him and felt my eyebrow rise. "I don't know… Do I want to know?"

Cadriel's smile could never be described as warm or nice or pleasant, not really. He was the sort of guy who only found humour in someone else's discomfort, pain, or general misfortune. But he was good at his job and he was the closest thing I had to a friend, aside from Thane.

His smirk now told me that someone was definitely heading for misfortune category.

"Kyle want to know," he said with a nod, pulling himself up on the bike seat to try to seem taller.

"It's a fucking shambles, down there," Cadriel chuckled, his eyes sliding down to the devilbum.

Kyles claws went over his mouth as he gasped.

"Let me guess, the Torture Fields have got lazy, there's a unicorn on the loose in the Asphodel Fields again, and Larry's group is terrorising them all?"

Cadriel kicked his head to the side. "Close."

"Kyle want to know about the puppy!" He bounced on his toes.

"Cerberus is fine, Kyle," Dad said as he swanned out of the mansion. He paused for a moment and clarified, "He *is* fine?" with Cadriel.

The Grigori nodded. "He's doing his job."

"Which is more than some of us are doing?" I finished for him.

"I would never disrespect the Lord of Hell, or his son," Cadriel said and, once again, I envied their ability to lie.

Dad either chose to miss it or just plain did. "Thank you. I mean, the last holiday I took was forever ago," he said as he started walking back inside and Kyle clambered up the stairs just behind him. "A devil's allowed to take a break. Comfort breeds complacency, I always say–"

"When have you ever said that?" I asked, but he wasn't listening to me.

"–and no one wants a complacent devil. What if we started torturing the wrong souls!" he chuckled. "Can you imagine the paperwork?"

I shared a glance with Cadriel.

"Bedlam in the Assignment Office," Cadriel said wryly.

"Exactly. Sometimes, it's like you're the son I never had. You sure you're full Grigori?" Dad waved his hand. "Of course, you are. What a stupid question."

"Are you all right?" I asked him, thinking the behaviour was weird even for him.

He turned, but looked slightly absent. "What? Oh. Yes. Fine. You boys have at it, then. Just try not to break too much, yes?"

He left us in the entry hall and I looked around. It was pure white marble everywhere, trimmed in the purest gold physically possible. Great gilt mirrors and paintings hung on every surface of wall. Stairs swept up grandiosely from the entrance. We wandered into a sitting room that was equally outlandish.

"Someone spared no expense," Cadriel commented as he helped himself to a couch.

"Yeah," I answered his unspoken thought. "I was wondering who he had to indispose, too."

"The guy really likes his parties."

"And his comfort."

"It's not every day your son gets married."

"On the subject of my reason for being on Earth…" I started awkwardly as I sat across from him.

"Mm?" Cadriel asked. "What about it?"

"I'm in need of a Best Man."

There was that smirk again, only I wasn't sure whose misfortune was coming. "I see. Well, you've certainly come to the best. Man is a touch insulting, though."

"And what makes you think I was going to ask you?"

"Who else would you ask?"

"Thane?"

Cadriel nodded. "You could, I suppose. But you won't."

"Why not?"

"Because Death isn't really Best Man material, is he? He's even further from man than I am."

I had to concede that. No one really knew what to classify Thane as. He was one of a kind.

"You might be right."

"I am right."

"So, you going to agree? Or will I be forced to go with a Best Miscellaneous Entity?" I asked.

"Who's the maid of honour?"

"Tilly."

He crooked one eyebrow. "Tilly?"

"Wren's sister."

Cadriel's face took on an expression I knew all too well. He didn't care what human it was as long as they were willing.

"But you keep your hands to yourself," I said firmly.

He threw his arms up. "What fun is that?"

"The kind that doesn't bring more unwanted attention to my wedding. Last thing I need is Azazel and his goon squad getting wind of you actually fornicating with a human. It's bad enough I'm doing it."

"Oh, don't be so hard on yourself," he said in much the same manner you'd tell someone not to throw themselves into the Hell Pit when you actually rather wanted them to. "You can't help you fell for a human."

I looked at him. "Hey, I was born damned. You quite *literally* fell for a human."

Cadriel's face darkened. "Some things are beyond even your ken, Nephilim."

Had he actually cared, I would have got an axe to the stomach. As it was, Cadriel just preferred not to think about his fall. It was different for all Grigori but, while the thought of the actual fall was painful, none of them regretted it.

"Will it just be the two of us then?" he asked me, obviously eager to change the subject.

"For what?"

"The wedding party."

"No. I was still planning to ask Thane"

"Death in a human wedding. A beginning, not an end," Cadriel mused. "Beautifully ironic. How are you planning to ask him?"

Getting hold of Thane in the afterlife had proven difficult enough. Now we were on Earth…?

"No idea."

"We could kill someone."

I frowned at him. "I like hunting as much as the next hellspawn, but I think gaol might put a dampener on the early days of my marriage."

"I can't imagine being separated for years made for a particularly good one, either."

"She only had weeks."

"So, now only the little human's feelings matter?"

"Ugh. Don't tell me you care about me?"

Cadriel scoffed. "No. Of course not. The more you suffer, the better I feel."

"We're still not killing someone."

"Can we try to kill you?"

I looked at him and frowned. "Pardon?"

He shrugged. "I just figure that the near-death of Lucifer's last Nephilim would get even Death's attention."

"And how's that supposed to help the early days of my marriage."

"You literally have eternity with her, Morningstar. You can spare some time out to get Thane's attention."

"And, if I'm still healing at the actual wedding?"

Cadriel shrugged again. "You'll go supernova before you let that happen."

"Now we're relying on supernova," I muttered as I got up and limbered up.

Cadriel had already decided he was going to try to kill me whether he had my permission or not. I may as well be ready for it.

But I wasn't ready for it.

Cadriel launched at me full force and sent us careening through the couch behind me and into the wall. The whole mansion shook with the force of our crash. His wings were out and he was in full fight mode. I looked into his eyes and saw he wasn't just gunning for blood.

"When you said try, I assumed–Shit!"

Cadriel picked me up and tossed me across the room. I smashed straight through the grand piano and landed on top of the debris. Something cracked, but I had no idea what it was. I coughed, but there was to be no reprieve.

The Grigori hauled me up off the floor before I even thought about getting up, punched me in the gut and sent me flying into the bar. The thing must have been saved solid because my whole body bent around it and barely made a dent in it.

"Ow," I breathed as I fell to my knees.

But still no respite. Cadriel kept coming for me. Finally, I managed to get a crack in and our fists crashed into each other and both our wings sprouted, sending a shock wave through the room and breaking a fuck tonne of glass.

From then it was a fairer fight. Barely. Cadriel was trying to kill me and I was supposed to be letting him try. But self-preservation's a funny thing. We were both bruised and bloodied and swiftly running out of energy by the time he landed a stellar kick to my chest and sent me sprawling across the floor.

He leaped and landed between my legs with a shard of glass pressed against the skin of my stomach.

"Just stick it in," I snapped, deciding to stop being a pansy about it.

"It won't go in," Cadriel said.

"What do you mean it won't go in?"

"Just…relax or something."

"I am relaxed! Put it in."

"Am I interrupting something?" came a familiar voice.

I looked around and saw Thane was leaning against the doorframe in full regalia. Thane spun his Scythe into nothing and threw back his hood as my father walked into the room with a, "What did I say about breaking things?"

"This is not what it looks like," I said carefully.

"That probably depends on who you ask," Cadriel said.

"You're trying to fuck him," my father said as Thane said, "You're trying to kill him."

They looked at each other and then back at us.

"I told you," Cadriel said to me as he dropped onto the floor next to me, looking about as exhausted as I felt, as the glass clattered from his hand.

"I'm still not sure which one it was," Dad said and I rolled my eyes at him.

"Kill. He was trying to kill me." I flopped on to my back.

"I'm all for channelling your excessive rage into something productive, son. But death is a touch extreme, don't you think?"

We all looked to Thane.

"Well," Dad amended. "Dying. Not…" He waved his hand in Thane's rather tame direction. "You know."

"We needed to get Thane's attention," Cadriel explained.

"Consider your mission a success," Dad said ruefully.

"Why did you want my attention?"

Cadriel and I were both lying in pools of glass and our own blood, breathing heavily. There was no sign of supernova. But we'd heal.

"I wanted to ask you to be my groomsman," I panted.

"Oh, neat," Thane said.

There was silence for a while.

"Was that…a yes?" Dad asked and I was glad I didn't have to speak.

"Oh!" Thane chuckled. "Yeah. Of course."

"Excellent," Dad said.

All I had the energy for was waving a vague high-five in his direction.

"That all you wanted?" Thane asked.

"Yeah," Cadriel sighed.

"Cool. Chuffed about the groomsman gig. Better get back to work, though. Reap you later, dudes." And he was gone.

"I hope you two are going to clean this mess up," Dad said pointedly as he picked his way gingerly around us and over to the bar to pour himself a drink.

Cadriel and I lay on the floor for quite a bit longer.

Wren

"Rumours are swirling that the devil himself walks the Earth," caught my attention.

"What?" I muttered, looking for the remote to turn the volume of the TV up.

The reported continued, "People are asking is this it? Has the apocalypse arrived? Is this the end of the world as we know it?"

The news cut to clips of Lucifer gallivanting around town. Hooning around in his red Lambo with the number plate that read 'DAMNED'. Posing for pictures while being entirely on fire and loving it. Hanging out with a K-Pop band. And…

"Is that Keith Richards?" Dad asked and I turned to see him walking in.

I shrugged. "Dunno. Is it?"

"I'm sure it is," Dad said.

"I thought you were all supposed to keep a low profile?" I said to Truman.

"As we are, ma'am. By law, humanity is not supposed to know about our existence."

"Is there a reason for that? Or is it just one of those arbitrary laws?" Dad asked.

"Well, sir, that depends on who you ask." Truman clasped his hands behind his back. "Many will tell you that humans don't really do well when faced with the certainty of the afterlife. There's something far more comforting about blind belief than certainty."

"Like if you know for a fact that there's a Hell, you're more worried that you'll end up there?"

"Much like that, sir, yes. Heaven seems less attainable when you *know* it exists. Hell seems more likely. There are those that will panic and throw themselves into worship in the hopes of getting into Heaven. Then there are those who've decided they're probably going to Hell anyway and lean into it."

"You say that like it's happened before," I said slowly.

"Many times, ma'am. Many times. And every time the being responsible gets a slap on the wrist and Earth's off-limits to all but the bare minimum of personnel."

"What does a skeleton crew of personnel look like?" I asked.

"The Grigori and the Fallen have very little choice, but they are strongly advised to keep to themselves. Thanatos of course gets free reign wherever he needs to be. Other than that, it's a strict no-go zone for a few years."

"Is that supposed to make people forget?"

"That is the general idea, ma'am, yes."

"So, humanity just gets left to their own devices?" Dad asked.

"In many ways, humanity is always left to their own devices, sir."

"I thought Lucifer and that tried to recruit people for Hell while angels and whatnot tried to keep people on the path of good?"

"You would be surprised at the resilience of humanity to police themselves in that manner, sir."

I snorted. "Are you saying we're just as corrupt as either side there, Truman?"

He inclined his head. "I'm sure I don't know what you mean, ma'am." There was a slight smile in his voice and I grinned.

"Of course, you don't."

"I thought you were meeting up with Harmony for lunch?" Dad asked me.

I looked at the time. "Oh, shit. Yeah. I'd best go. I can still borrow your car?"

Dad pretended to sniffle. "My little girl, about to get married and still borrowing my car," he teased.

I huffed, "Is that your weird way of telling me you're buying me a car for my wedding?"

"No!" Tilly cried as she wandered in. "You're buying her a car?"

Dad laughed. "No one's getting a car they don't buy themselves. Certainly not from me or Mum. Besides, what's Wren want with a car in Hell?"

The mood sobered somewhat at the suggestions of my departure.

I tried for a laugh. "No, the tunnels aren't really suited to driving."

"Indeed, ma'am. And I would hate to think what his devilness would do if he was in charge of road rules," was Truman's addition.

I could see we'd all envisioned Lucifer being in charge of road rules. I doubted we all had the same idea, but all of them were as terrifying as they were funny.

"Get some milk in the way home, will you, Wren?" Dad asked as he fished the car keys out of his pocket.

I nodded. "How much?"

"Couple of two litres, I think."

"No worries."

"Thanks, darl," he said gruffly as he hugged me swiftly.

Dad wasn't an unloving person, he was just a little bit weird about physical affection. And I knew that wasn't made any easier by me moving out soon.

"Need a lift anywhere?" I asked Tilly.

She shook her head. "I'm good thanks."

I realised I hadn't seen Kyle or Ignacio for a while.

"I believe Ignacio is in the shed, ma'am, and Kyle went with Master Drake again."

I nodded, trying not to let it bother me that Kyle was spending more time with Drake than me. It was silly to feel that way. Kyle had known Drake his whole life and he'd known me for a few months. It made sense he'd missed Drake and wanted to spend time with him now they were together again. But I missed his little red, leathery grin.

I headed out, telling those at home to call if they needed anything else, and drove to the mall to meet the girls.

Pippa, Leah, Bonnie and Eliza had been my friends since we were in year eight. Unlike Harmony and Tilly, they didn't know all the ins and outs of who I was marrying; Harmony had just blurted out at school to them that I was engaged. I'd hesitatingly told them that all our giggled teenage fantasies had come true and he was the old next-door neighbour I'd married when I was five. Past that, they mostly didn't seem to care I was getting married at eighteen. It was just decided that we all liked him very much and our parents were really excited about it which made it more than okay in their eyes.

But they're being okay with it made me feel weird about it. I almost needed someone to question me about my logic so I could defend myself and remember all the reasons I was doing it. Instead, as soon as I sat down with them at the café, I was inundated with wedding questions.

"Have you said yes to the dress?"

"What kind of flowers are you having?"

"What about food?"

"Is there a colour scheme?"

"Have you registered for gifts?"

"Where are you going to live after?"

It seemed never ending. And the only one I had answer to was, "The date is, set. Yes?"

I nodded to Bonnie. "Six weeks."

"I can't believe we haven't even met him. This is like a fantasy!" Eliza sighed wistfully.

I was rethinking my blanket ban on letting Drake make people okay with me marrying the son of the devil. It would solve so many problems if I could just tell them everything and have them get over the freaked out, 'the devil's real?' part of it.

"How about that Lucifer guy, huh?" Harmony said, looking at me pointedly.

I wasn't sure if I was telling her to keep her mouth shut or blow the whole thing wide open and save me some hassle.

"Oh my God! I know," Pippa laughed.

"I doubt he has much to do with it," I muttered then realised I'd become more hellspawn than I'd realised.

"What?" Bonnie asked and I shook my head.

"He's something, isn't he?"

"He is."

"Do you think he's actually the devil?"

"I dunno. They can do some pretty fancy things with special effects these days."

"Yeah, but like he seems so sure of himself. And Bobby said that he saw him in real life and he actually juggled those elephants."

I shared a look with Harmony. Of all the things I'd heard of my father-in-law doing, juggling elephants wasn't one of them.

"Like…" I started. "Balloon elephants?"

Pippa shook her head. "Like elephants, elephants. I can't even imagine how you'd be able to juggle elephants."

"He'd find a way," I said without thinking.

"Do you actually think he's the real devil?" Eliza asked.

I shrugged. "Let's just say I don't *not* believe it."

Eliza, Leah and Bonnie laughed, but Pippa nodded and said, "Me either."

Maybe my father-in-law dicking about Earth was going to be to my advantage after all and it would make it easier to tell my friends exactly who Drake was without any mystical assistance.

All my life, I'd naively assumed that falling in love and getting married would be easy. Not the wedding planning part. I was well aware how stressful that could be and I'd expected that. What I hadn't expected was the other stuff. Stuff like how I basically had two lives now.

Tyring to be human Wren at the same time as being Drake's wife was tiring. It was hard. It was like I was constantly lying to most of the people around me and I couldn't find a balance. When we were in hell, it was easy. Humanity wasn't supposed to be kept a secret. The time difference was well known. But on Earth?

How did I explain to people that I'd gone away for three of their days, lived a month, and fallen in love with a Nephilim without sounding crazy? I didn't want Drake to have to mess with their realities and make them okay with it. I wanted to be able to talk to all my friends and family about him like a normal person.

I was definitely rethinking our deal.

He'd flat out promised me that the only time he'd done it was when I was telling my parents about my weekender. Everything else, he assured me, was all me unless I said otherwise.

Now I just had to work out if my peace of mind was worth relinquishing my friends' freewill.

Drake

My father was using his time on Earth to potentially disastrous consequences. So far, he'd made sure to meet all of his favourite celebrities.

I'd had to endure an hour alone of him recounting how wonderful Kylie Minogue was. The guy had a full-on crush on her and had wandered around his totally inconspicuous mansion with literal stars in his eyes.

There were a bunch of them I hadn't even known about and I had no idea when he'd had the time to discover them either. But he was known for popping up to Earth to deal with personal business now and then.

And, of course, he'd caught up with Keith for old time's sake.

Not only did I have to hear about so much of it, but he was all over the human's news. The devil walks the earth? They thought the fucking apocalypse was coming. There was panic, and weird cults had started popping up.

Doomsdayers were suddenly trending on social media with #ApocalypseNow, #DevilWalkstheEarth, #DevilAmongUs and #DevilWalking.

Naturally, Dad was having a grand old time with the whole thing. It hadn't taken long for most of the hashtags – something Wren and the Contemporary Life consultant had tried explaining to us to little avail – to go from spreading panic and doom to just making my father and his various escapades go viral. People were desperate to get a selfie with him and show the world they'd met the real devil.

"I can promise you that, while someone's world is going to be rocked, the world at large is safe," was something he had legitimately said to someone.

Not that anyone believed him. But as his shenanigans became more commonplace, it seemed like humanity still believed the end days were nigh, they were just a little less worried about when it finally happened. After all, Lucifer was fun. How bad could the end of the world really be? I swear, at least a million people were suddenly solely invested in making sure their lives led them to the endless party that they expected in Hell when they died.

They'd get a rude awakening when they realised the only person my father ever entertained was himself, and at other's expense. But humanity didn't see that Lucifer. They saw the guy who set himself on fire. They saw the tiki version. They saw the guy zooming around in his fancy cars, a leggy blonde under each arm.

He finally had a captive audience and it suited him to keep them interested.

Meanwhile, I was stuck with Samyeza.

"The least you could do is leave enough space for the holy spirit," I said to him.

The big Grigori leader was taking the whole 'on my six' thing far too seriously.

Unable to break the habit of a thousand lifetimes, I'd taken up residence in Dad's mansion. It was big enough that, even when he was home, it usually took actually looking for each other for us to see each other. It also had the benefit of having more privacy for Wren and me when she came over. And, the house was protected in ways only the ruler of Hell could provide.

And yet, Samyeza had suddenly forgotten the meaning of the term 'personal space'.

I ran into him more times than I could count because he was always just behind me.

"The holy spirit doesn't need physical space," Samyeza retorted.

I huffed, "Tell that to all those kids who went to Catholic schools." Something caught my eye about Dad on the television again. "What's the paperwork going to be like for this?" I asked the Grigori, not really expecting an answer.

"That highly depends upon the state in which he leaves things."

I looked at him. "What's that mean?"

"It means that the devil is quite possibly the only being in creation capable of introducing the reality of the afterlife's existence without drastically altering the course of humanity's future."

"You serious?"

"The expectation is that the council is meeting and deciding what to do about him. Be thankful for the age of superheroes and social media hoaxes. It has made humanity both more open to the mystical, and also more sceptical."

"So, those laws…?"

"May change. It may be irrelevant. Eventually, Lucifer will return to Hell and everything will calm down. Either Earth will once again be placed under embargo, or it will not."

I wasn't entirely sure what he meant, but the door opened and distracted me.

"We have to make some decisions, Drake," Wren said vehemently as she walked into the sitting room.

"About what?" I asked, thinking it was a bit much to hope it was about what position to try out next.

"About the wedding."

"Like what?"

"Flowers. Colour scheme. Food. Gifts. What we're going to tell people when they ask where we're going to live. And I still need to finalise dresses, and mine."

"I'm sure my dad won't mind doing it for us."

She glared at me and dropped on the couch. "Hey," she said with a nod to Samyeza, as used to his presence now as the devilbums.

I looked around. "Where are the boys?"

"Ignacio's been in the shed for the last week and no one's allowed in. Truman's helping Mum." She looked up at me. "I thought Kyle was with you?"

I scanned the room like he was just suddenly going to appear.

"Kyle is in the pantry," Samyeza said.

"What's Kyle doing in the pantry?" Wren and I both asked.

"He has discovered Nutella. I have been told it goes well with Wizz Fizz."

Wren shook her head. "I don't even want to know." She looked at me again. "Are you going to sit down?"

I sat on the couch next to her. "Sitting. Now what?"

She sighed. "Some decisions maybe?"

"What do you want to start with?" I asked her.

"With me not making all the decisions," she said and I could tell something was bothering her.

I kicked my head towards Samyeza and he excused himself from the room.

"Come here, beautiful," I coaxed, gently encouraging her to slide onto my lap.

She came not unwillingly. I put my arms around her and nudged her nose with mine.

"Talk to me," I asked.

"Why don't you just read my mind and find out?" she grumbled, watching where she played with the front of my t-shirt.

"Because you don't like it when I do that."

Her eyes found mine and I saw the love in there. It was swimming with annoyance and exhaustion and confusion. But it was still there and that was all I needed.

"I'm just…" She sighed. "I'm tired, Drake."

I nodded. "I can tell. Do you want to go upstairs?"

She gave me a pointed look. "Really? I'm not sure sex is the answer."

I gave her a wry smirk. "I was implying a lie down."

"No. Not that kind of tired."

"Talk to me, Serenity."

She lay against me and I rubbed her back gently.

"How do I be your wife and a human? I just… I don't know who I am anymore. I feel like it's ridiculous to be planning a wedding straight out of school, but also like it's the most normal thing in the world. Here I am, planning to move to Hell like that's a thing people just do."

"You…do still want to get married?"

She sat back and looked at me. "Of course, I do."

I nodded. "Because…" I cleared my throat. "I would understand if you were having second thoughts."

Wren's eyes went wide for a moment. "No! Shit, no. Never. Because… You're not, are you?"

I held her more tightly. "I'm on the fence about this whole wedding thing, but not about you."

"Then why are we—"

I lay my finger over her lips. "Because our parents want it. Kyle wants it. And, most importantly, you want it." I nudged her gently. "You want the white dress and the family and friends. And, as much as I'd rather take you home and spend the next twenty years in bed with you, I would much prefer to meet at the end of a church aisle."

Her eyes went wide for a totally different reason this time. "Did anyone think about that?"

I frowned in confusion. "About what?"

"The church."

"What about it?"

"So many things. But first on the list would be can you even go in a church? Can your dad? What about Cadriel?"

I chuckled, my lips brushing hers. "We'll be fine."

"How?"

"If it was a problem, you would have heard about it already."

"How is it not a problem? Isn't Cadriel going to burst into flames as soon as he steps through the door? What about the devilbums?"

I took her face in my hands to get her to look at me. When she finally did, I saw panic lancing through her eyes. I tried not to laugh.

"We're fine. There are only a few churches on Earth where that would be a problem and Cadriel knows a guy. A priest."

She nodded like she was thinking about that. "Oh. Okay."

"You don't mind?"

"Don't mind what?"

"About the church? Was there somewhere you had in mind?"

She shook her head. "No. No, I didn't have anywhere in mind. No one in the family has a church they're particularly attached to or anything."

"Okay. Well we can cross one thing off the list then," I told her.

"The church?"

I nodded. "The church."

She took a deep breath. "Okay. Good. One thing down and a thousand left."

I nuzzled into her neck and she laughed. "And are we allowed a reward for every decision we make?"

"What were you thinking?" she asked.

"Oh, I think you know what I'm thinking, baby."

I knew my eyes were red so I pulled away and let her see them. She bit her lip against a smile and I didn't need to read her mind to know what she was going to say.

"Okay," she laughed finally. "Okay. We can have a reward."

I spared no time taking her up to the bedroom. I wasn't sure if, strictly speaking, a reward was supposed to take three times longer than the decision itself, but I wasn't complaining.

7

Wren

"This one would look *wonderful* on you," Lucifer said as he held a dress up to his body on the other side of the shop. "Hm?"

"I'll try it on." I shrugged and went back to looking at the racks.

"When's the wedding?" the shop assistant asked me.

"Uh…five weeks," I said.

"Five weeks? That's not a lot of time. We usually prefer at least five months' notice not…" She paused. "Of course, five weeks is fine."

I heard Harmony laugh and turned to my father-in-law.

"Lucifer!" I hissed.

He shrugged in that nonchalant innocent way he had.

"Oh, let him have his fun, Wren," Mum said with a smile. "It's sweet he wants to be involved."

I rolled my eyes, knowing it was futile to argue. "I'm not sure 'sweet' is the right word to describe him."

"What about this?" Tilly asked and I turned to her.

She was holding up a silk slip-dress. It was the sort of thing I'd wear the night of the wedding, not for the ceremony. Not that other people wouldn't manage to pull it off... In the sense that they would look good in it and no one would think they shouldn't be wearing it. Not in the new husband pulling it... I cleared my throat.

"I'm not sure that's really me," I said slowly, not wanting to seem rude.

"No. For me and Harm."

"For me?" Harmony asked, sticking her head back around a rack to see. "Oh, I like that."

"White's very traditional," Lucifer nodded appreciatively.

"White for the bridesmaids?" Tilly asked. It had taken a few weeks, but she was finally – mostly – normal around the non-humans now.

Lucifer nodded. "Oh yes. Colour's quite a new thing."

"Why did they wear white?"

"To confuse any who might wish the bride harm on her wedding day."

"Someone like the devil for example?" Harmony asked cheekily.

Lucifer grinned at her, definitely putting the devil in devilish. "For example."

"Did it work?"

Lucifer turned to look at her. "Was I confused because they were all in white?" he asked like it was the stupidest thing he'd heard

Harmony nodded. "Yes."

He opened and closed his mouth a couple of times, turned back to the rack, and said, "Maybe once or twice."

"Well, it sounds like a legit strategy," Tilly said. "Confuse those Fallen guys if they crash the wedding."

I didn't hate the idea of white bridesmaid dresses, but I doubted the Fallen angels would be terribly fussed by which bride they stole or killed or whatever. They'd probably just cover their bases and go for all of us.

"Marrying the son of the devil with a wedding party all in the purest white?" I asked.

Lucifer smirked at me. "How deliciously vainglorious of you, dear."

"What do you think?" I asked Mum.

She nodded. "I think it's a good idea."

I'd been hesitant to let Lucifer come dress shopping with us. And, when I say I was hesitant, I of course mean that I knew I couldn't say no. It *was* nice, in a really weird way, that he wanted to be involved. But I knew that you didn't really say no to the devil. Which sort of made it feel less like a choice and more of an obligation.

Once again, I felt trapped between my expectations and my reality. I wasn't even sure when we'd really come up with the date of the end of January. There'd been some discussion about it at that first family dinner where Lucifer met my parents, but I couldn't remember whose idea it was or why I'd agreed to have it so soon. I supposed, when it was really just for appearances, that it had seemed silly to wait longer than necessary.

But I didn't have time to feel put out about the stressful directions my life was pulling me in because I had dresses to choose and not very much time in which to do so.

"I want to see you in this one," Harmony said as she walked towards me with it.

It was a full-on ballgown design with such a huge skirt that she had to walk like a cowboy to hold it in front of her body. The torso was bedazzled something fearsome, but I'd made a promise to myself that I wasn't going to pooh-pooh anything. I had no idea what I wanted, so I would take every suggestion.

I nodded and the sales assistant came into the change room to help me into the dress.

"This one is very popular with the young ladies," she told me. "Everyone dreams of being a princess, don't they?"

I wasn't sure I had, but that hadn't stopped me becoming an actual princess. True, it was of Hell and I don't think that's what she meant, but didn't make it any less right.

She helped me out of the cubicle and I didn't have to see myself to know it wasn't me. I felt like I was in constant danger of falling flat on my face. Except I wouldn't fall on my face because there was a butt load of tulle to cushion me.

As soon as Tilly and Harmony saw me, they broke out into very poorly hidden giggles.

"Oh, dear," Lucifer said as he looked me over.

Mum shook her head.

Harmony covered her mouth.

And Tilly exploded with, "You look like a giant marshmallow!"

"Yes," Lucifer said. "And Kyle's quite decided he likes marshmallows."

"How about something else?" Mum asked, getting up and going back to the racks.

I stepped awkwardly up onto the block and looked myself over. I did look like a giant marshmallow and not in a good way. The waist was too low for my shape, making me look cylindrical until the explosion of tulle from my hips.

"What are you thinking?" the shop assistant asked.

"The waist I don't think is sitting right. And something slimmer. Not so…poofy…?" I wasn't sure what I was saying.

But the assistant nodded. "I think I've got some ideas."

I toddled around uselessly while the others helped the assistant find dresses, then we'd dress me in one and go again.

I tried on a yellow-cream mermaid tail dress that I could barely walk in.

There was a similar trumpet style that was a bit easier to walk in, but still made me feel like I was in desperate need for a wee.

There was a crisp white, silk sheath style that felt far too revealing.

"I think I need…more…" I said, although it sounded more like a question.

Next came an a-line dress that I was quite happy with.

"Something still feels a little…?"

"Empire," Mum said and I looked at her.

"What?"

"An empire waist."

"Of course!" Lucifer said. "And I'm thinking lace?"

"Oh, nice," the assistant said.

I knew on the first empire waist that it was the right design. Finding the right rest of it was a bit of a task. But, finally, we found something nice and simple. Something traditional but with contemporary flair, something me.

"It's perfect," Mum said wistfully.

Tilly and Harmony nodded.

When I looked at Lucifer, he gave a single nod. "Perfect."

8

Drake

I hadn't realised how many varieties of flowers there were. I hadn't realised that each one had a different meaning. I hadn't realised how fucking long it took to choose which ones to have at a wedding.

But it had. It had taken hours. So many hours. If one thing came of it, it gave me some more torture ideas. In fact, if something other than my being married to Wren came of our wedding, it was that I had quite a few new ideas to spice up some of my torture techniques I felt were getting a little old and stale after a couple of millennia. The worst bit about the job was the monotony, after all.

We'd finally decided on calla lilies in white and dark purple. By the time we'd answered a thousand questions about how we wanted them for bouquets, boutonnieres, church bunches, table decorations, and every other possible use for a flower you can think of, I was about ready to shove them up the florist's arse. But I put on my only slightly grumpy face and stuck it out for Wren.

When we finally got back to Wren's parents' house, the television was on even though no one was watching it. Samyeza, who was getting better about remembering what 'personal space' meant by the week, sat in the corner of the room and minded his own business. And Wren and I went over the huge lists of caterers and menu option.

After a while, the television cycled back to the latest news headlines. No surprise when one of my father's many faces turned up.

"Can you tell us, once and for all, is the apocalypse here?" the reporter asked.

"No, no," my father laughed. "There are no end days in sight. Everyone's safe."

"Then, other than having a *wicked* time, why is the devil really walking the earth now?"

Dad leant forward and tapped the side of his nose. "I'm just here to help plan a wedding."

The reporter woman seemed very interested in that. "It must be a very special wedding for you to come to Earth to be involved."

He nodded. "It is."

"Can you tell us whose wedding it is?"

Dad nodded. "I can."

There was a pause before the reporter asked, "Will you?"

Dad chuckled as though his (feigned) absent-mindedness was adorable. "Sorry. Yes. Yes, I will. It's my son's wedding."

"Your son?"

Dad nodded.

"The antichrist is on Earth?"

My wandering attention was brought sharply back to the television to see Dad's answer as well as hear it.

Dad spluttered. "The...? No. Dad, no. Drake's not the antichrist." He shook his head forcefully. "No."

"But the antichrist isn't merely fable?"

Dad looked stumped for the first time in his very long life. "Ah." He cleared his throat. "Well, that all depends on your definition of antichrist, I suppose."

"The being responsible for raising Hell on Earth."

"Oh, him," Dad smiled awkwardly as he rearranged in his seat. "Sure. Um. No one knows that one."

"But your son isn't the antichrist?"

"No. Hells, no. Drake had a mortal mother."

"He's half human?"

Dad nodded. "That's the way these things go."

"And his future wife?"

"Full human. Wonderful little creature."

"So, your son lives on Earth?"

Dad waved a hand at all the queried implications in her voice. "He usually lives with me. But I decided that a Prince of Hell–"

"Not that kind of prince," I muttered and Wren squeezed my hand.

"–needed to be wed. Well of course, my son's a clever thing – chip off the old block and all that – and decided he already had a wife. She came down to Hell for a bit, now they're getting married properly."

"I see. And by properly, you mean a satanic ceremony? Will there be sacrifices?"

"By Hells, no. Full white wedding. Church. The works. All we're missing now is the virgin." He winked at the camera and I felt Wren freeze beside me.

"He did not…" she breathed.

I tried to hide my smirk. "Just tell the world you weren't a virgin?"

"Oh my God," she mumbled, burying her face in her hands.

I leant towards her. "He still doesn't have much to do with it."

She snuck a look at me through her fingers and I saw her cheeks were bright red. I took hold of her wrists gently, not yet trying to coax them from her face.

"Like anyone's going to know it's you anyway."

"I cannot believe him." She paused and dropped her hands. "No. I can *totally* believe him."

"It's fine. How many humans are still virgins when they get married these days?"

"Not the point!" she said.

"Then what is the point?"

"There's a difference between people assuming that we're…sleeping together, and them being told we are by your dad."

I shrugged, not getting it. "How?"

She blinked. "Because… It's… I'm still human, Drake. I still have human feelings and emotions. Shame for one."

I frowned. "You're ashamed about having sex with me?"

She shook her head. "No. But…it's our business what we get up to. I don't want people thinking about us… Like that…"

I'd forgotten how prudish humans could be. Wren and I had fallen for each other in Hell. Where the rules didn't apply. No human rules applied in Hell. We had no need for shame because that was it; there was nothing coming along after for us to worry about what others thought of us or what our actions meant. It was too late.

Although, there was one particular field down there dedicated to just humiliating souls, so maybe that wasn't quite right.

It was probably a good thing I was immortal and bound to Hell anyway.

"What does it matter if they know? Let them. There are far worse humans in this world than someone who has sex before marriage," I said.

She looked at me like that was definitely not the point. She huffed a held a hand up in front of my face. "Just… Ugh." As she walked out, she shook her head and pulled her phone out of her pocket.

"What did I say?" I asked the ever-present Samyeza.

He looked at me over the newspaper he'd been pretending to read. He even had a small pair of pince-nez glasses perched on his nose.

"I have always been amused by humanity's insistence in innocence as a virtue. As though the human race's continued survival did not rely solely on carnal activity. Closed doors have always been important to them."

I looked after Wren and sighed. "Okay. I get that–"

"Understanding the theory and understanding her feelings are two very different things," he said.

"Are you my guard or my shrink?"

"I'm whatever I am needed to be." He put the paper down and looked at me fully. "Do not mistake my thoroughness for enjoyment of my task. I informed Lucifer how stupid it was to let you run amok on Earth. But he will not be swayed when he wants something."

"Especially when it's a party."

Samyeza inclined his head in agreement. "While logic dictates that Azazel would not dare send someone to kill you, that very same logic pales in the face of determined zealotry."

I nodded. "You know Azazel well, then?"

"We have met many times in battle since the beginning of creation. Even before God's favour shifted to the hearts of man, not all angels believed in the same things. Peace is – shall we say – a construction of humanity."

There was a lot about my family's history that I knew. But there was obviously a lot more that I didn't know. When you were the son of the devil, you started to feel pretty certain that you were only told the pieces of information he wanted you to know. Even with beings like Thane and Cadriel.

"So, you think Azazel's coming for me?"

"I think it a miracle he has not already."

"He knows what my father would do to him if he did."

Samyeza inclined his head. "True. The problem with zealots is that they are willing to die for their beliefs. It makes them incredibly irrational and even more dangerous."

"What's the likelihood he comes after Wren?"

"Difficult to determine. That will depend on many things."

"Like what?"

He shook his head. "Fear not for her, Drake. Not only is she strong, but she has the might of Hell at her back. She would be a last resort at best. We will not allow it to get to that."

"Because it's your job?" I challenged.

A ghost of a smirk hinted at Samyeza's lips. "Because she is the human who bravely walked into Hell."

"I'm pretty sure she was scared as all Heaven."

He nodded. "And that makes her even braver."

I frowned. "How?"

"Because she knew every risk, and yet she still chose you."

As annoying as it was to have a shadow constantly follow me around, the guy had a good point. I'd known Wren had been brave in walking into Hell. Stupid maybe, but brave. And I was incredibly glad that she had. But I'd never stopped to realise that her walking into Hell and knowing most of the worst of what she'd face made her even more incredible.

I looked at Samyeza and he gave me a polite yet curt nod.

Maybe the guy wasn't so bad, after all. Maybe if I worked with him rather than against him, we'd both get through this better off.

Wren

There was a tall, gorgeous woman with her arms around my husband. And he was hugging her back.

She had long, thick auburn hair rolling in waves down her back. In it there were flowers and butterflies. Her eye makeup was dark and her lips were dark brown, complementing her olive skin marvellously. She should have looked like a twelve-year-old going to a school disco. She didn't. She looked like a bloody goddess. And she was all over my man.

"Um… Hi," I said loudly.

Drake was still as cool as the proverbial cucumber as he painstakingly slowly took his arms from around that delicious specimen of woman and turned to look at me.

He was smiling! He was… It wasn't much by most being's standards but, for him, it was a bloody beacon. Whoever this woman was made him smile in a way I never had. He looked positively carefree. Or as carefree as he was able. His posture was the most relaxed I'd ever seen it when he was awake. He didn't seem quite as on edge, not quite ready for a fight at the drop of a hat.

"Wren!" he said to me, putting a hand behind her back.

What was that? Possessive? Obsessive? Had Drake ever put his hand behind my back like that? Okay, maybe he had. Maybe he had and I was quite clearly overreacting to just how damn perfect this woman seemed. I felt significantly lacking in comparison.

"Is this her?" the woman asked Drake.

Drake nodded. "This is Wren."

Why didn't he sound happier or prouder or…whatever it was you were supposed to be like when you were introducing your wife to someone? Did he, and my jealous haze had just missed it? What was wrong with me?

"Wren. This is my stepmother, Persephone," Drake said to me, his arm still behind her back.

All I could do was nod. The word 'mother' in no way made me feel better about her.

"Oh, it's so wonderful to meet you, Wren!" she said warmly, stepping forward to hug me.

I put my arms around her stiltedly, looking to Drake for an explanation. Her hug was kind, it was welcoming. I felt bad for not returning it, but it was just a little beyond me just then.

As Persephone finally pulled away, I said, "I thought Esther was your stepmother?"

Persephone laughed. It was light and airy and wonderful. I hated it. "You should know by now these things aren't quite that simple."

I wanted to believe she wasn't being condescending. Nothing about her seemed condescending. She gave off that vibe of just being…nice. But I couldn't help feeling like it was all a front.

I scoffed. "No. Of course, I do." And I did, but I still made it sound so much like I was bullshitting my way through belonging with Drake. Which annoyed me further.

Persephone was still smiling warmly. Were her cheeks not sore? "Like all mythology, Hades is…complex. Do you know the story of how I came to be his wife?"

I didn't want to shake my head. But I had to. "No."

Persephone looked at Drake and tutted. "Really, *huiós*? Have you shared *anything* with her about the family?"

"There's a lot of it to go through."

"Oh, a lot of it. And I suppose you were too busy with other things, were you?" she teased. She tapped him on the nose and looked to me like we were sharing the joke. I didn't feel like I was sharing the joke.

Drake looked cheekily sheepish for the first time I could ever remember.

No.

Wait.

I had a fragment of memory from when we were little. His mum had told him off for…something my mind hadn't held onto after thirteen years. He'd had the same look on his face then. That 'whoops, you caught me, but you love me too much to really punish me, right?' look.

The word 'mother' was starting to make me feel a bit better. Maybe.

She was so pretty. All light warm and light and fresh somehow.

And, holy Heaven, she did look so nice.

Persephone nodded at Drake. "Mm hmm. I thought so." Her light brown eyes turned to me with a mischievously bonding sparkle in them. "I see you and I have some catching up to do, darling."

All I could do again was nod. Only, this time, I was speechless from wonder rather than trying not to say something rude.

"Let's suffice to say that eating anything in the Underworld curses the shit out of you," she continued.

I looked to Drake quickly and saw him clearing his throat awkwardly.

"What?" I asked.

"Okay…so–"

"*Huiós*, you didn't?" Persephone tapped him on the head. "There are plenty of brains in there, Drake. Use them."

He shrugged. "I wasn't thinking."

"Yes, I see that."

"Sorry," I interrupted. "What do you mean cursed?"

Persephone settled into the sort of look that you knew a serious explanation was coming. "If you eat of the food of the Underworld, then you must reside there for at least three months of the year."

"Six," Drake said.

"Watch yourself, boy," Persephone told him and I was sure it was an inside joke. "Either way, once you eat of the food of the Underworld, you're bound to it." She pointed between us. "I assume it's worked out all right. But I'm interested in what you would have done if she hadn't literally walked through hellfire for you, *huiós*. Kudos, by the way," she said to me. "I admire a brave woman."

"You heard about that?" I asked, feeling all giggly suddenly.

She nodded. "I did."

Drake smirked. "Persephone has her own network of spies and confidants—"

"Oh," she tutted. "Don't call them spies. They're my…"

"Special friends?" Drake finished for her.

Persephone waved a hand. "Don't give Wren a bad impression of me before she's had a chance to get to know me."

Drake put his arm around me and pulled me close. "Wren is more than capable of making up her own mind without anyone's influence."

"Well, that's obvious. Or she wouldn't have chosen you." Persephone winked at me and I couldn't help but smile.

"Are you staying for the wedding?" I asked her.

She shook her head. "Alas, I'm due in the Underworld."

"You have to go?"

"I do."

"Because you ate food from the Underworld?"

She nodded. "Every winter is my payment."

I looked around pointedly. "But it's summer."

"Here, yes."

I nodded. Duh. Different hemispheres. "But it's the end of December…"

She smiled. "You might start your seasons on the first day of the month. The northern hemisphere starts theirs on the solstices and equinoxes."

"So, you have to go soon?" Drake asked.

She nodded. "I do."

"Hey, upside. Dad will be busy up here so you won't have to see him."

Persephone looked at him like she'd already considered that. "I know."

"You and Esther going to have sleepovers and pillow fights?" he teased.

Persephone pouted. "Oh, at the very least."

"Esther will love it."

"Behave yourself, *huiós*," she warned him. "You keep that wife of yours safe."

Drake nodded. "I will."

"Good. I expect you to be a better husband than your father."

"I plan to be."

"Wren," she turned her smile on me and I returned it. "It was a pleasure to meet you. I hope we can spend some real time together."

I nodded. "I'd like that."

And I found I was telling the truth. I was quite happy to get to know Drake's stepmother better. This one, anyway. Esther still freaked me out.

"I might see you when you come home," she said to us both then she was gone in a puff of dark ochre smoke that smelled of fresh spring air and flowers.

Drake pulled me to him, wrapping me up warmly.

"So, I'm cursed now, am I?" I asked him.

He had the decency to look apologetic. "Persephone doesn't talk about it much. In the desire to…make you happy…it slipped my mind."

"It slipped your mind, or you didn't care enough at the beginning to think of it?"

He looked up and bit his lip. "Uh… Good question. Maybe both?"

I smiled. "Well, at least you're honest."

His eyes dropped back to mine. "I can't lie."

"That isn't the same thing and you know it."

He nodded and sucked his teeth. "True."

"So, exactly how does this cursed thing work? I have to live in Hell for at least…how long each year?"

He wrapped his arms around me. "Three months was the original story. Some dudes later on decided it was six. Persephone seems to do fine on three months. She's gone for winter, then comes back to Earth along with the new growth of Spring. They used to say it was her absence that caused winter–"

"How does that work for the southern hemisphere?" I interrupted.

He smirked. "I couldn't tell you. I'd have to ask her. Maybe there's a southern equivalent goddess?"

It hit me then that we'd never talked about living arrangements. How stupid was I to be planning a wedding to a guy without talking about living arrangements? And it wasn't like he just lived in…like…France. He lived in Hell. I lived on Earth. Didn't I? Maybe not. Had I just sort of assumed that we'd live in Hell with no thought of my friends or family? What had I planned?

"What?" he asked.

"Oh, you're not going to check for yourself?" I teased.

He nudged my nose with his. "I could. I thought you didn't like it?"

Honestly, I didn't hate it. But that might have been because he seemed to try not to invade my privacy as often as possible.

"I appreciate you don't abuse the power."

"Then I'll do my best to keep out of there."

"Thank you."

"But, if I'm going to do that, you're going to have to talk to me…" he said softly, his lips brushing mine tantalisingly.

"I was just…"

"Having second thoughts?"

I shook my head, my nose rubbing against his. "No… I was just thinking about how we'd never talked about where we'll live. How we'll live. I've just kind of gone along with this whole thing thinking that love is all that matters."

"It isn't?"

"Have you thought about it?"

He shrugged. "Not really."

"Are we supposed to just live in our room in Hell for the rest of my life?"

"Well…" he said slowly.

"What?"

"You don't age in Hell, Wren. It's going to be longer than a lifetime…"

The way he said that, I was sure he didn't like reminding me in case that's what made me start rethinking this whole thing. But it didn't bother me, so on some level I must have already realised that and accepted it. Which suggested I had just thought we'd live in Hell. But what the Heaven would my friends and family think about that?

"Did you…?" he started, then cleared his throat. "I mean, what do you want to do?"

I shrugged. "I don't know. I know you can't live on Earth. You've got obligations that you can't leave for even just a few days on Earth. I'd never see you. But what happens if I live in Hell with you? How often would I see my family? Harmony?"

He sighed. "That can be arranged as often as you like. I'm sure Dad would get them their own doorway to get in safely. It would definitely give you more time with them."

"And as they age?"

"I'm sure we could arrange some sort of nice torment for them when they die?"

His voice was deadpan, but his blue eyes twinkled. I couldn't help but laugh.

"Thanks, but no."

"Think of it this way. I didn't see you for twelve of your years and I lived millennia down there. As far as all of you are concerned, it's the best way around. If you lived in faery…" He scoffed.

"Bad?"

"Terrible. Works the opposite. I lived a millennia of Earth's years, it'd be even more compared to those fae bastards. They might have lived a few months in that time."

"Really?"

"Really."

It didn't sound all that bad to me really. The living in Hell thing, I had no interest in going to Faery. If I didn't age, then it wouldn't matter how long I lived between them visiting. Even if it was years for me and weeks for them, it would work. By the time they aged and died, I'd have had plenty of opportunity to see them. It seemed ideal, to be honest.

"So…if we lived in Hell…?" I started.

"Mmm?"

"What would I do all day? Would we just live in our room?"

Drake wrapped his arms around me tighter. "You could do whatever you wanted all day. You could manage Larry's a capella group. You could run Waterboarding Wednesdays. You could help train the baby devilbums. You could keep an eye on Dad and make sure he pulls out as little musical numbers as possible."

"What if I want to do more than that? Go to uni? Be productive?"

"Training the baby devilbums is a legitimate full-time job."

I tilted my head to the side. "That honestly doesn't sound awful."

"Did you want to go to uni?"

I sighed. "I don't know. I applied, of course. But nothing ever really felt…right."

"Maybe that's because you were destined to be my wife?"

There was something about that that made me feel like less of a failure for not having a full life plan at eighteen. "Maybe." I looked at him. "I suppose we'll work it all out, won't we?"

He nodded. "You will never want for anything, Wren. You decide you want to go to uni? I'll make it happen. But there are also plenty of things you can do in Hell."

"Things that are safe for poor mortals?"

He grinned. "Things that are safe enough for fragile mortals. There are even quite a few philosophers, mathematicians, tutors and teachers, writers, historians…quite a few of the people involved in the big historical events… They can teach you whatever you want to know. We can probably even get Thane to drop some of the Heaven-bound souls by to give you a lesson in something if you'd like."

Everything about that sounded far more interesting than going to uni to do a generic degree and end up with a giant piece of expensive toilet paper and still no idea what I wanted to do with my life. Maybe Drake was right. Maybe I'd never felt quite right on Earth because I wasn't meant to be on Earth. Maybe I had always been destined to be Lucifer's daughter-in-law.

Drake

Christmas on Earth. It had been almost literally forever since I'd had one, let alone a Christmas at all – celebrating the birth of my uncle had never really been Dad's favourite holiday. Which didn't stop him leaning fully into it while he was, as he called it, topside.

There was a massive tree, decorations through the house, and a party with all the friends and family. To be honest, mostly Wren's friends and family considering Dad and I didn't really have anyone we'd care about inviting to celebrate my uncle's birth.

But with everyone relaxed, I should have known that was when he'd come.

Wren was inside dancing with the devilbums and Harmony, and I needed a breather. It was the first time I'd managed to give Samyeza the slip. With our newfound…understanding, shall we say, I felt slightly guilty about causing his post to be abandoned. But I really needed the fresh air and a moment to myself away from the constant questions about the wedding.

It had been so long since I'd just stood outside and breathed.

Earth air wasn't like Hell air.

In Hell, it was this constant hot, muggy feeling. You could almost feel it in your mouth if you breathed too deeply. You got used to it. It wasn't like it made it difficult to breathe, unless that was your eternal punishment. It wasn't stifling, until you stood on Earth and breathed in the fresh, light air they had on offer.

When I'd come back for Wren, I'd been too distracted to notice. I'd had a mission. I'd been focussed. But when we spent hours just sitting in the backyard talking with our parents over a glass of wine or bottle of beer, it became more noticeable.

It brought back memories of my childhood. Nothing really concrete, it had been too long ago in my memory for that. But there were snippets, feelings. Things I'd forgotten about. Things I thought I'd lost forever before Wren brought them all back to me.

So, of course, it was while I was feeling relatively at peace that something hard cracked into the back of my head and I found myself flat on my face with someone pressing me into the grass.

"Thought you could run from me forever, did you?" was hissed into my ear.

I couldn't move to see who it was, but I didn't need to in order to read his mind.

"Azazel."

"Picked up a few tricks from your father, I see, bastard."

I lay still, waiting for the moment his pressure on me slackened. It was inevitable that he'd get overly confident that he'd bested me. I just had to wait him out. My mind whirled as I tried to evaluate my options.

As far as I knew, Azazel was the strongest of all Fallen – Grigori and regular fuckers alike. Which meant he had the power to beat Samyeza. And I could barely beat Samyeza on a good day.

"How did you get past the wards?" I asked, more stalling for time than I was interested in troubleshooting the flaws in Dad's security system.

"Your father has been absent for many years. We have new tricks up our sleeves."

"I'll remember to book you for Kyle's next birthday, then," I grunted as he squashed my face further into the grass.

"Funny little things. Nephilim," he mused.

"No funnier than any other jerk with wings."

I felt a blade dig into my cheek and slowly drag down. "I wonder. Is pain your trigger, bastard?"

I didn't know what he was talking about, but I'd sparred enough with Cadriel and Samyeza to know that keeping your opponent talking was a brilliant distraction. "Oh, I don't know. I like pain as much as the next guy, but I wouldn't call it a kink."

"Hm…" he murmured in my ear. "The son of the Morningstar is likely to be used to pain. It would need to be something…" The blade drove into my back and I forced myself not to react. "Exceptional."

"Maybe you're just not my type," I suggested.

Azazel was heavy. And his knee was planted in my back with his hand on my face. Nothing about the guy suggested he was going to get cocky and overconfident any time soon. Without guaranteeing I could get the upper hand if I shoved him off me, I wasn't sure what my options were.

"Anger perhaps…" he whispered.

Now I really didn't know what he was talking about.

"Those Nephilim usually kill themselves long before now. Volatile little shits."

"If I killed myself, I'd have just ended up in the same place. Seemed like a waste of time to me."

He chuckled, but it was mirthless. "I wonder if it's lust, then. Does the idea of your precious *wife* laid out and waiting for you set you off, I wonder?"

"You don't talk about her," I warned him, my voice icy.

"There it is," he purred. "And I'm afraid we can't have that."

Wait. Was he talking about going supernova?

Supernova wasn't something I turned on or off. I had no control over when it came or went. When I'd first heard about it, I'd spent months trying to force myself into it to no avail. I'd made Cadriel beat me to a pulp. I'd submitted to my own personal Hell. I'd tried forcing it out with anger, pain, sadness. Nothing had worked. It was like, the more you wanted it, the further away it got.

The only time it had been close was after Wren left. I'd been worried that she'd be hurt because of me. I was worried Azazel would use her to get to me. But that wasn't really working as a motivator just then because, once I was dead, Azazel wouldn't care anymore.

He had me. He had no reason to go after Wren. Killing an innocent human wasn't going to get him back into Grandad's good books.

"The last one still didn't stand a chance," Azazel told me. "You are nothing, Nephilim. You can't even protect your own *wife*."

"You wouldn't hurt her," I spat.

"Wouldn't I? Way I see it, I kill two birdies with the one stone. I'll slice her pretty little throat then you'll put yourself out of my misery."

I saw red. I felt red. Everything was hot and fire.

"Drake!" I heard Samyeza call, but I was too far gone.

With an explosive power I didn't know I possessed, Azazel was blasted backwards. The only problem was, everything else around us was levelled. The tree we'd been next to splintered into a trillion little slivers.

I swayed on my feet, feeling nausea sweep my body.

"I think I went supernova," I muttered as I fell and Samyeza caught me before the blackness enveloped me.

Wren

The whole party stopped as Samyeza helped Drake walk in.

In the space of a heartbeat, Lucifer went from congenial party host to the Lord of Hell.

"What happened?" he demanded.

"Azazel," Drake rasped.

Fear lanced through me as I looked Drake over better. He looked terrible but he was already healing. His skin was covered in thick cuts and his clothes looked singed. Samyeza didn't look much better, but at least he didn't look like he was about to pass out.

"Here?" Lucifer asked.

Samyeza nodded.

"What happened?"

"Let me get him upstairs. Then we can talk."

Lucifer nodded absently. "Yes. Good. Wren, go with him, will you?"

I vaguely registered the party breaking up as I followed Samyeza and Drake upstairs. Samyeza got him into his room and onto his bed. Drake grimaced as he shifted himself.

"Do not leave the house," Samyeza warned. "Serenity!"

I looked at him. "What?"

"Do not leave the house."

I nodded numbly. "No. No, I won't."

"Stay with him. I will be downstairs if you need anything."

"Of course."

The Grigori left us, closing the door. I dropped onto the bed next to Drake and he smiled at me softly.

"You should see the other guy," he said.

"Did *you* see the other guy?" I asked, surprised he'd managed to walk away.

Drake tapped the side of his head almost drunkenly. "I can't turn it off right now, Wren. Just so you know."

I blinked. "I doubt I'm going to be thinking anything I don't want you to hear," I said, then immediately pictured him pulling me onto him and slowly making love to me. I cleared my throat as he chuckled roughly.

"I could be persuaded," he said.

"I think you've got more important things to worry about," I told him.

Drake shook his head. "Nothing's more important than you."

My heart fluttered happily and I tried not to smile on hearing that. It didn't feel right to be smiling goofily while he was hurt.

"I'm healing," he said grumpily. "I'll be fine."

"What happened?" I asked.

He took my hand, lacing his fingers with mine. "Azazel took me by surprise. I swear the bastard's insane. When I thought that was it – he'd kill me and you'd be safe – it was okay. At least you'd be okay. He wouldn't possibly hurt an innocent." He laughed but there was no humour in it. "But then he threatened you. Fucker was going on about triggers, wanted me to go supernova. He found it. My trigger." He winced as he pulled himself to resting on his elbow to look at me. His eyes glowed bright red as he searched my face. "It's you, Wren. The idea of your death is too much for my body to handle…"

I cupped his cheek. "Shh. It's okay. I'm fine. You need to rest."

"I did it, Wren. I went supernova. He said he'd kill you and I lost it."

As much as those words elicited a range of feelings in me, I firmly reminded myself now was not the time to explore them.

"Why not?" he asked. His voice was low and husky, no longer just weary but full of lust.

"We've been through this. You're injured. That is hardly the time to be…together."

His chuckle sent a pleasant shiver up my spine. "What if I promise to be gentle?"

"I think I'd be able to take it rougher than you right now."

"Is that a challenge?"

I shook my head. "No. It's not." But, of course, I had a momentary rogue thought about how that would go and I knew he caught it.

He took my cheek in his hand and brought me to him. My lips found his like it was as natural as breathing. He coaxed me into lying down with him, only pausing to wince a little.

"See. Injured," I said, making to pull away, but Drake's hand latched onto my wrist and, when I looked into his eyes, I'd never seen him look so serious.

"I'm not sure if you've gathered this, Serenity," he said slowly. "But I believed you were going to die tonight. Properly die. Never see you again die. Lost to me for eternity die. I hesitated against Azazel for fear I couldn't overpower him, but you gave me the strength to. It scared the Heaven out of me and all I'd really like to do is be with my wife. Please."

"I don't want to hurt you."

"You won't hurt me," he said gently.

Drake lay back against the pillows and he pulled my arm towards him. I couldn't help but smile as he enticed me to climb on top of him. He stayed lying down and let me go to him to kiss him. One hand went to my neck like he felt the need to keep my face near his in case I tried to pull away from him. The other one started on my back and slowly trailed down to my arse.

As we kissed, our bodies moved together, awakening a desire in me that only he could. I wanted more, but I was conscious he was hurt.

"Take it," he growled against my lips and need coiled tightly in the pit of my stomach.

Usually, I felt squeamish at the idea he could read my thoughts. This, though, seemed like it might have hidden benefits. I felt him smile as he kissed me and I knew he'd heard that as well.

"You are a princess of Hell, Serenity," he said, sitting with me still straddling his lap. "You walked through Hell. Take what you want."

Well, when he put it like that, it was difficult to think of a coherent argument as to why I shouldn't.

He helped me with my zip and we fumbled to get my dress off.

My fingers skimmed the hem of his t-shirt and he lifted his arms to let me pull it off him. He was still healing, but he didn't wince, even when I traced my fingers over them lightly.

"You can withstand so much…" I whispered.

He tipped my chin to make me look at him. "I couldn't withstand losing you."

A thrill ran through me every time he said something like that. I'd meant it when I'd told him he made me feel powerful. He made me feel like I could do anything I wanted, anything I could think of. He didn't just give me courage to face my fears, but he made me believe success was possible.

I gently pushed him back onto the bed, not hiding in my thoughts what I was planning. I watched him smirk as he was more than prepared to do what he was told. I made quick work of undoing his pants and getting them off him. His full naked glory was lying bare before me, unashamed and ready.

My clit tingled in anticipatory excitement of feeling him in me. But there was something I wanted to do first.

As I took him into my mouth, my hand ran up his stomach. He took it and held it tightly as he breathed deeply. It was times like that that I wished I was the mind-reader. I would have loved to know what he was thinking.

"I'm not sure what I'm thinking is appropriate for refined young women," he grunted as I sucked him.

"I'm not sure I'm a refined young woman," I told him.

Before I could wrap my lips around him again, he gently pulled me up his body.

I looked at him in interest and he just shook his head at me as he reached for my bra clasp. He dropped it and my undies on the floor then pulled me into his lap again.

Slowly, I lowered myself onto him. His strong arm wrapped around my waist and mine around his shoulders. He kissed me as I rocked my hips against him. It was a different feeling. It wasn't just sexual gratification building, it was deeper. I felt it in my soul, if such a thing was possible. I felt not only desired but protected, not only desire but protective. Something seemed to swirl around us, tangible only in how just out of reach it felt.

Drake let me do most of the work and I told myself he'd react worse if he was in too much pain.

"I'm fine," he murmured against my lips and I felt his smile.

"You're sure?"

He nodded as he held me close, our foreheads resting against each other. "I can't lie, remember?"

"That's not the same as telling the truth," I replied.

My voice came unsteadily as the pulsating rhythm in my clit started tightening and coiling pleasantly like the beginnings of a rumbling climax. My pace increased and his arms tightened around me. Our eyes locked as I rode him and I felt that deep connection, something that called to me. It was what had me determined to walk through Hell. It was what had me knowing that my destiny lay with him.

"My pain is minimal and easily drowned out by more pleasurable feelings," he said.

I nodded, feeling easily distracted by the pleasure building in me. "Good–"

"Shh." He kissed me. "Don't worry about me. Concentrate on you."

"I can do both."

I felt his smile and I saw it in his eyes. "Just come for me, baby."

I cupped his cheek and kissed him deeply. The rolling of my hips became more frenetic and desperate as he rubbed me in all the right places. It didn't take much longer for the coil to snap and radiate through my body. I held him close as I moved slower, more languidly as I rode it out.

He wasn't far behind me. I felt him tense under me and his hands gripped my skin firmly. I didn't have to be a mind reader to know that it had been different for him as well.

We lay down and he nestled me against his body. We didn't speak before we drifted to sleep, but I could feel the steady beating of his heart almost against mine.

Drake

Cadriel and I were sparring in the entrance hall of Dad's behemoth of a mansion. There was something oddly pleasant about seeing blood splatter across the pristine white tiles and the gold accents. The fact that Cadriel had just spit blood all over Dad's precious Mona Lisa was all the better.

"You know," he started as I helped pull him off the floor and out of the debris of what used to be a priceless piece of furniture from Catherine the Great's private collection. Dad did indeed have a thing for the Greats.

"I know you've got a tiny dick," I huffed a rough chuckle.

His eyes darkened. "By comparison, that would make yours microscopic, would it not?"

I kicked my chin toward him. "At least I don't keep mine in my hair."

Cadriel turned to the mirror and had a look. With a wry smirk, he pulled the little wooden decoration from Catherine's chair out of his hair and flicked it away.

"Any other genitalia where it shouldn't be?"' he asked me.

I shook my head. "Nothing out of the ordinary. That cock on your forehead's growing, though."

"And here I was, about to suggest we have a meeting of the bridal parties. I was even going to behave."

"I'm definitely in," Thane said as he appeared out of nothing but the darkness that creeps into the edges of your vision when fear grips your body.

He thrust his hood back and lost most of his ethereal quality.

"What are you doing here?" I asked.

"I'm keeping an ear out for any time either of you mentions the wedding." He picked an ear out of his sleeve and waggled his eyebrows. "Heh? Huh?"

"Put me out of my misery," Cadriel droned.

Thane frowned. "Some souls appreciate me."

"Some souls are stuck with you taking them to the other side," Cadriel said. "There's a difference."

"Kyle appreciate Thane," he said and we all turned to see him in the doorway to the kitchen. He had a jar of Nutella in his arms and a spoon in his hand.

"I take it he's not so into apples anymore?" Thane asked.

Kyle grinned at Thane as he shovelled another spoon of Nutella into his mouth. Then he held the jar out to him.

"Thane want some?"

"Uh…" Thane started. "No. I'm all okay for Nutella. Thanks though."

"Okay," Kyle said. "Kyle get the Wizz Tingles."

Thane looked at me in question as Kyle headed back into the kitchen. "What are the Wizz Tingles?" he asked, much like he didn't actually want to know at all.

"Fruit Tingles in Wizz Fizz," Cadriel explained.

"Are they actually words?" Thane looked at me.

"It's tangy sherbet lollies in tangy sherbet," I said when Cadriel didn't elaborate.

"So, sugar in sugar…with sugar?" Thane looked towards the kitchen. "You know I don't babysit, right?"

I shrugged. "He got Kyle on them, not me."

"Wizz Tingles!" Kyle said as he came back in with a bowl. He had a fair amount of Wizz Fizz on his face and sounded like he'd already started on the Fruit Tingles.

Kyle held the bowl up to Thane, who looked at me like he'd really rather not be a guinea pig.

"Do you even eat?" Cadriel asked.

"What do you mean?" Thane replied.

"It wasn't code. What I said. Do you eat?"

"I can. I just don't have to."

"Huh," Cadriel huffed. "Do you like eating?"

"Depends what it is."

I pointed at Cadriel. "If you make a pussy joke, I will shoot you."

"Kyle likes pussy," he announced. "But Kyle didn't eat Mrs Finster's." He shook his head so his leathery ears flapped and the three of us very mature beings all snorted.

"That's not what it sounds like," I told them.

"I guessed," Cadriel said wryly.

"Kyle funny?" he asked hopefully.

I nodded. "Sure. Kyle funny."

"Like Thane. Wizz Tingles, Thane?"

He nodded. And thus, I was witness to the first time Death tried Fruit Tingles and Wizz Fizz. It started an eternity-long love-affair he was never quite able to break.

"You were talking about the wedding," Thane said as he licked his finger clean of the Wizz Fizz.

Cadriel shrugged noncommittally. "Sort of."

"I believe the Grigori had a suggestion."

"It is common practice for the bridal parties to get to know one another," he said. "I was merely offering this as an option. As the Best Angel, I thought it my place."

"That's right," Thane said. "And I said I was in."

"Just like that?" I asked.

"Don't you have souls to reap or something?"

"They'll wait for…a little while," he answered,

"You mean no one will die for a full hour or something. What happens to the world then?"

"We all explode," Thane huffed, then waved a hand at the very concerned Kyle. "No. It's fine. There's… I'm not needed like *all* the time."

I'd never known if Thane was the kind of being who could or couldn't lie. He was as old or older than Grandad and Dad – not that he looked or acted like it – and I wasn't sure if he even really knew what he was. He didn't have the power of my family, but they had very little to no power over him. It had been the point of many heated discussions between us in the past.

"Okay," I said slowly. "Say we have a meeting of the bridal parties. What's your suggestion on activities?"

"I suppose we're not even going to consider an orgy," Cadriel drawled nonchalantly.

I glared at him. "What have I said about fornicating with humans and my wedding?"

Cadriel held up his hands defensively. "Okay. I was just checking."

"Why don't you ask Wren?" Thane asked.

"Because I hate to think what a bunch of humans would come up with," Cadriel answered for me.

"They might surprise you."

"So might clowns, I still don't want to get into bed with them."

Thane looked at him. "But you *do* want to get into bed with humans."

Cadriel nodded. "Exactly."

"Wait. What?" Thane looked at me. "Do you get what he means?"

I shrugged. "I've stopped trying."

Cadriel sighed loudly. "It's a metaphor. I wouldn't want to get into bed with whatever useless activity a human would come up with, much like I wouldn't want to get into bed with a clown."

I nodded to Thane. "I'll ask Wren what they want to do."

Wren

I can't say I had any idea what bowling with a Nephilim, a Grigori and Death would be like, but it sounded like the start of a bad joke.

A Nephilim, a Grigori and Death walk into a bowling alley...

It was a good thing I'd never aspired to be a comedian.

I didn't really know why we'd been so eager for bowling when Drake told me about doing a wedding party introduction and asked us to pick an activity. We'd discussed the movies but thought that was a bit weird if we were supposed to be getting to know each other. And just going for dinner seemed awkward if no one got along and we spent the whole time not talking. So, bowling had seemed like a good thing to do if we wanted to talk or we didn't want to talk.

When Harmony, Tilly and I walked in, they were already at a lane and weighing up balls. The girls and I got our shoes and headed over to them.

Cadriel and Drake were both wearing jeans and t-shirts. Drake's were darker and Cadriel's lighter. Thane, though, was wearing chinos with his t-shirt. Compared to the two others, he looked small and weak.

"…fingers in these holes and then I…throw it down there?" Thane was asking.

"Who's that?" Harmony hissed at me. I looked at her to see which one she was looking at.

"That would be Thanatos."

"Thanatos…" she said, trying the word out kind of weirdly.

"Also known as Thane. Also known as Death."

"The Death?" Tilly asked. "Like robes and scythe and ferries you to the other side? That Death?"

I nodded. "Yup. Hey, guys."

"It's less of a ferry," Thane said. "That's kinda more Charon's gig."

"Oh, I met him," I said with a smile. "He seemed…okay."

Drake rolled his eyes. "He let you fall in the Lethe."

I shrugged. "I'm okay, aren't I?"

Cadriel looked at me weirdly. "She fell in the Lethe?" he asked.

Drake nodded. "Mostly."

"They caught me before full submersion."

Cadriel nodded. "That'd be why you're marrying him then."

Drake shoved Cadriel, but it seemed a mostly companionable action.

Harmony keyed in everyone's names into the machines. It was boys in one lane and girls in the other, but we weren't competing between lanes, as became very obvious very quickly.

"All three of them are beating us," Harmony complained.

"You're winning your game," Thane pointed out.

"Are we not playing you?" Tilly asked.

As Drake stood up for his turn, he said, "You'll never win that way," and spared me a wink.

"Rude," Harmony said.

"And yet," Tilly started, "in no way wrong."

I looked at the scoreboards again and noticed that the boys were indeed at least doubling our score. Each.

At the end of the first game, I was perfectly happy coming last out of the six of us. Particularly because there was conversation moving between the two groups. Nothing worthy of noting in the annals of history or anything, but friendly banter, a cheer for a good ball, general chit chat.

It was the second game when everything devolved into madness and the boys started getting worse scores and the girls started getting better ones. It was also around the time that we ordered a couple of bowls of wedges. There was slightly less bowling and more eating and talking going on as we took longer and longer pauses between turns.

Drake released his ball with the perfect amount of precision and speed. But just at the last minute, Cadriel coughed. I looked over and noticed a very odd hand gesture for someone coughing.

"You piece of…" Drake cried.

I turned back to the lane and saw his ball make a very last-minute beeline for the gutter, missing absolutely every pin. Cadriel's next cough was a very poor attempt at hiding a snigger. Thane grinned and even Tilly laughed.

"I don't really think that's in the spirit of the game," Thane told Cadriel.

Cadriel shrugged. "If they didn't want us to cheat, they should have warded the place."

Harmony sat forward. "That stuff works?"

Cadriel mimicked her lean. "Define stuff."

"Like there's actual wards and things that humans can use on…not humans?"

"Of course. We may not be bound by Earth's laws, but we are not lawless."

"So says the Grigori, the most lawless of us," Drake commented as he walked over. He smacked Cadriel upside the head and the Grigori moved over for Drake to sit next to him.

"What do you call Thane, then?" Cadriel retorted.

"Thane doesn't count."

"Why not?" Harmony asked and I could see Thane was very much counting in her books.

Tilly and I shared a smile.

"Because he belongs everywhere and nowhere," Cadriel explained. "He's older than the laws themselves."

Thane's cheeky grin completely belied that statement.

"So, wards protect humans?" Harmony asked.

"Wards protect whoever they're for," Drake said.

"Upstairs has wards against downstairs. Downstairs has wards against upstairs," Thane said.

"And the Fallen have a whole deal as well," Cadriel added.

"This is like you mentioned with the church thing," I said.

Drake nodded. "There are a handful of humans who have warded their churches."

"Any we know?" Tilly asked.

The three of them shared a look.

"Vatican for one," Cadriel said and looked mighty annoyed.

"That's what you get for fucking about with nuns," Thane chastised.

"Nuns?" Harmony snorted.

Cadriel shrugged. "Something like that. I'd like to see them prove anything."

"I hope you boys are planning something a little tamer for the buck's party," Harmony said.

Cadriel nodded. "We're almost all sorted. Between me and Samyeza we've got a typical buck's party planned."

I followed Cadriel's gaze and saw Samyeza over at the bar. He nodded to me.

"Which reminds me…" Drake started and I looked back to him. "He wants to send a Grigori on your Hen's do."

I blinked. "He wants to do what?"

"It's just a precaution."

"So…Grigori come in female?" Harmony asked.

"We're fallen angels," Cadriel said like that was an answer.

Harmony looked at him and, when he didn't explain what that meant, she asked him, "So?"

"So…no, they don't come in female."

"Why not?"

"Because there are no female angels."

"What?" Tilly, Harmony and I chorused.

"How?" Harmony asked as Tilly said, "Why?"

Cadriel shrugged. "Take it up with the patriarchy. That is not within my purview."

"So, we'll have a cock in the hen house, you say?" Harmony asked, looking Thane over pointedly.

"Why is it a hen and a buck?" Tilly asked.

"Yeah," Thane mused. "Why not cock or doe?"

"It could be a cock party," Drake said.

"Yeah, when?" Cadriel sniggered.

"When it's yours."

"It's nice to know males are the same in other species," Tilly commented dryly.

We chatted for a while longer, then the wedges were gone and we got a bit more serious about bowling again. When we were both waiting, Drake wrapped his arms around me and looked at our friends.

"I'm surprised they get along," he said.

"I'm surprised Cadriel's kept his hands to himself, from what you've said."

A wry smirk crossed his lips. "I told him in no uncertain terms what the rules were."

"Yes. Because he's quite obviously a stickler for the rules."

"Are you okay with having a Grigori on your hen's night?" he asked suddenly.

"Why?" I asked, suddenly suspicious. "It's not going to be Cadriel is it? I assumed you'd need him for your bucks with all his excellent ideas."

Drake nodded. "It won't be Cadriel. I don't know who Samyeza has in mind."

I shrugged. "I mean, I don't care. It might look odd, but I don't much care."

"Then be thankful I talked him down from two."

"He thought two would be good?"

Drake looked at Thane bowling and Cadriel cheating, again. "He suggested we could probably find a succubus to help, but I wasn't sure how you'd feel about that."

"A succubus on my hen's night?" I asked. "Well, seems semi-appropriate. How would you feel about that?"

"Like you were safer."

I nodded. "All right. A succubus and a Grigori it is."

"Thank you." He smiled at me and leant down to kiss me.

"Get a room," Harmony laughed.

"You get out of our room," I teased back.

14

Drake

Piss ups were common place for Nephilim, demi-gods, celestials, demons, and/or miscellaneous entities such as Thane. Buck's nights, on the other hand? Pretty rare.

But the boys had insisted.

After all, how many chances did a group of inhuman bastards get to have a buck's night on Earth. We'd be saved if we didn't take full advantage of it. And we couldn't very well have that.

I'd been too young when I'd left Earth to really know what a buck's night involved. But my quick catch up of all those horrible rom-coms for winning Wren over had shown me what to expect from Cadriel – who spent a lot more time on Earth than anyone I knew – and Thane – who'd reaped more than a couple of guys during a buck's party. Samyeza had been around the longest out of all of them and I knew, even though he was technically there as security, he'd have had plenty of input to the planning.

It might have been a small party compared to others – how was I to know – but we could hardly have got blokes like Larry or Neville up to Earth to joins us. Cadriel had made me promise we could do a proper Hellish 'sindig' when we got back full of blood, gore, death and destruction. I'd told him I'd assumed it was a given.

Samyeza and Cadriel were in the middle of a heated discussion about where they were going to take me next. Thane and I stood around as they argued, neither of us having any idea of the specifics. Cadriel mentioned the name of some place and Thane nodded.

"Reaped a guy there once," he said, pointing to the others. "Seemed nice."

"The guy?"

"No, the place. Heart attack."

"The place?" I asked, confused.

Thane shook his head. "No, the guy."

That made more sense, but Cadriel had made sure that sense wasn't going to be the theme of the evening.

"Fine!" he finally shouted. "You win."

Samyeza's grin was anything but humoured. "That is why I'm the boss," he said simply.

"Lead the way then, *boss*," Cadriel muttered.

Samyeza turned and, after flipping his retreating back the bird, Cadriel followed him.

Thane stuck his hands in his pockets and then we followed the others as well.

I might never have been near one on Earth, but I knew the signs of a strip club when I saw them.

"Of course, the Grigori bring us to a strip club," I said ruefully.

"The amount of lust swirling around those places?" Cadriel practically licked his lips like he could taste it. "I'd fucking live in one if I could."

Samyeza nodded to the bouncer and we walked in. It was dimly lit and I felt the music thumping before I heard it. Samyeza found us a table and Cadriel got the first round of drinks.

It had to be a testament to my feelings for Wren that I wasn't bothered by the strippers. Sure, they were decent to look at. But I had much more fun watching my comrades enjoy them while I ate an endless supply of chicken and downed yet another beer.

Thane was *sans* robes once again and looked like a normal – if slightly sickly – member of the living as one of the strippers gave him a lap dance. He caught my eye and spluttered chuckles.

Cadriel was likewise engaging the services of a young woman on a pole, after he'd relieved the man next to him of the contents of his wallet.

Even Samyeza wasn't quite as dour as usual. But he was a Grigori with half-naked humans waving their goods in his face, what did you expect? Well, the special something Cadriel had picked us up had kicked in. For all of us.

It was more potent than the nectar of the gods on mortal men.

It was more dangerous than every drug known to man being mixed together and injected directly into your major organs.

It had the power to bring literal gods to their knees. It had the lot of us giggling like school girls.

"You know…" I told Cadriel lazily, stifling another chuckle. "You know what?"

"Nah," he replied, a wide grin on his face. "What?"

"You want to know?"

He nodded. "Tell me. Yeah. Tell me."

I sniggered and shuffled closer to him. He leant towards me eagerly. "You know Wren?" I asked him.

He stopped to think about it for a moment. Then nodded wildly. "Yeah. Yeah, I know her."

"Yeah. I'm gonna marry her."

Laughter spluttered out into chuckles. "Duuuude!"

I nodded. "I know."

Realisation dawned in his eyes. "Duuude! It's your buck's party!"

I nodded. "Duuude, it is!"

"I do *not* believe that Drake-fucking-Morningstar is getting married," Thane huffed as he dropped into the seat beside me. He leant towards me and Cadriel. "To a human," he whispered like it was a big secret. He tapped his nose and nodded. "Yup."

"I'm the best man, you know," Cadriel said.

Thane nodded and picked up a glass. "I know," he burbled into the liquid as he drank. "I'm the…" He hiccoughed. "I'm the groomsman. Do you know who's pretty?"

I shook my head. "No. Who?"

"Harmony." Thane nodded. "Harmony is pretty."

"Wren's pretty," I said, laying my chin in my hand.

"Yeah, but Wren's yours." Thane pointed at me.

"She is." I nodded. "She is. Because I love her."

"Duuuuude!" they both exclaimed excitedly, throwing their arms in the air.

I felt a weird flutter in my heart and spluttered a drunken laugh. I pointed at myself in case they'd forgotten who I was. "I love her."

"You love her," Cadriel teased.

Meanwhile, Thane was trying to remember the words to the 'K-I-S-S-I-N-G' song.

"First comes… Wait… Wait… I've got it." He nodded once. "First comes being dragged to Hell, then comes–"

We all burst into laughter.

"I did do that," I laughed. "I did kinda drag her to Hell."

Thane pointed at me with as steady a glare as he could muster. "She did also kinda choose it," he reminded me.

I nodded. "Yeah. True." I huffed, feeling weirdly elated and surprised. "I love her. Like, *love* her, dudes." I sat back in my seat. "I didn't even know we could do that."

Thane leant so far towards me he was practically lying on the table. "*I* didn't even know we could do that. Can we do that? That's so cool. You love her lots, then?"

I sighed. "She's fucking amazing."

"She walked through hellfire for you, dude."

"I know!" I breathed.

"Cade…Cade…Cade!" Thane suddenly said.

"Yeah?"

"Drake needs another hit," Thane chuckled.

I shook my head. "No. No. I'm good. I couldn't even tell Wren I loved her. That shit is strong, man."

Cadriel chuckled roughly and held up the glittering bag. "She did me good this time."

Thane sighed wistfully. "She won't even talk to me after last time."

Cadriel and I snorted.

"Yeah," Cadriel said nodding as he reached into the bag. "You can't tell Veritas the truth is dead because you reaped it!"

Cadriel and I dissolved into sniggers and Thane huffed a laugh.

"Yeah… My bad."

Cadriel held his finger under his nose and took a snort of the pure truth Veritas had given him in honour of us celebrating my upcoming wedding. Then he passed the bag to Thane, who followed suit.

"I believe he actually told her that 'Death is coming for the truth', waved his scythe at her and fell off his horse."

Thane shrugged as he passed me the bag. "She'd just hit me with a whole bag of the stuff. I was high and thought it was hilarious."

"It was hilarious," I reminded him.

I looked at the bag and thought why not. After all I was only getting married once…twice… To one woman.

Either way, we had the whole night to ourselves and nothing to do except wallow in whatever excess our depraved minds could think of.

I held up the bag. "To a Nephilim falling in love."

"With a human," Thane added.

"And giving us an excuse to party," Cadriel finished.

I took one more snort and felt truth zinging through me. It made my brain tingle and my veins electrify. I looked at the boys and we started laughing again.

15

Wren

I didn't know any eighteen-year-olds who'd had a hen's night, and I certainly didn't know any human whose guests included two supernatural guardians in the shape of one Grigori and one succubus.

Aarin much the same as most of the – two? – Grigori I'd met, with a dark scowl and watchful eyes. He was dressed in jeans and a long-sleeved t-shirt with the sleeves pushed up. His muscles bulged and I wasn't the only one who had a hard time keeping my eyes off him.

"Are all Grigori really attractive?" Tilly asked me.

I shrugged. "Based on my limited experience, yes."

"Well, they're angels, aren't they?" Harmony said. "Aren't they supposed to be like the perfect specimens? It stands to reason humans would find them hot."

Tilly was still staring at Aarin, but she shook her head. "Remember when it wasn't normal that stuff like angels existed and humans were the superior sentient beings in our lives?"

"Humans have never been the superior sentient beings," Penoris – preferred name on Earth: Pen – said with a wry half-smile.

The succubus was exactly as you'd imagine a succubus to be. She was tall and lithe, with voluminous hair that hung in perfect waves around her face. Her body was curvy and sensual, and even I was feeling hot and bothered around her. She was wearing huge heels and a cocktail dress that managed to pull off sophisticated elegance while still showing a Heaven of a lot more skin than I thought I'd ever be able to.

"Just because you did not know we existed, does not mean you have not always been inferior," Pen continued.

"You know what she meant," Harmony said glibly.

She was, out of everyone, still totally blasé about everything. I was dragged to Hell to be Lucifer's daughter-in-law? Cool. I fell in love with the devil's son? Fine. I decided to marry him right out of school? All good. Kyle became totally infatuated with her? Aw. Goes bowling with Death? He's cute. Has a succubus and a Grigori on her best friend's Hen's do? Awesome.

It was beyond me how she was so okay with it all, but then she'd always been the one who could just go with the flow.

As well as Harmony and Tilly, and our guardians, Pippa, Eliza, Leah and Bonnie were with us. We were all walking down the street, following Harmony's GPS to the next bar.

"Okay. Google tells me, if we go down here, we'll pop out across the road from it," she said, pointing down a side alley.

"It's a little dark isn't it?" Tilly asked.

"Where's your sense of adventure? Where's your sense of freedom?" Harmony cried.

I scoffed, "Pfft. I walked straight into Hell. We can manage a slightly creepy-looking alleyway in the middle of town."

Tilly shrugged. "Okay. But I'd like it known that, if we get murdered, it's your fault."

I nodded to her. "Deal."

As one, we all stepped into the alley. Harmony and I went first, Aarin and Pen brought up the rear, and the other five shuffled along between us. Everyone but Aarin were treading carefully in the mostly-dark to make sure no one rolled their ankles – heels were precarious sober, let along after a few drinks.

The noises of the main roads behind and in front of us seemed muffled as we moved further into the alley. A gust of chill air buffeted us, odd for the time of year. Goose bumps flared to life across my skin and I shivered. An impending sense of doom was sneaking into my previously buoyant heart. I linked my arm with Harmony's and noticed I wasn't the only one holding on perhaps tighter than necessary.

No one spoke and the silence started to feel deafening.

Suddenly there was an ominous rustling behind us, sounding unnaturally loud against the quiet. It was a noise that sounded suspiciously like wings. I turned quickly, my heart racing.

Aarin looked at me like he was trying to work out what had me freaking out all of a sudden. Pen strolled beside him, perfectly confident in her monstrous heels despite the uneven nature of the path. Tilly and the others were safely wandering along still.

No one was missing. No one was hurt. Everything seemed fine.

Once all nine of us were standing in the brighter lighting of the road, I breathed easier. There was a collective self-conscious laugh as though the tension hadn't been just me. But I suppose, when you know things like demons and devils really exist, it makes it easier to fear them.

"That one," Harmony said as she pointed across the road.

Everyone followed her to the curb and waited for a break in the dribbling traffic. The group stepped into the road and that was when all Heaven broke loose. Quite literally, because Hell had nothing to do with what happened next.

There was an inhuman shriek from behind me.

A number of very human screams came from all around me.

Great buffeting wind swirled around us angrily.

Metal crashed against metal.

Alarms blared.

Blinding light flashed all around us.

I blinked hard to try to clear my sight and work out what was going on. Noise came at me from all sides and all I could hear were the noises of panic and terror. My heartrate spiked and I forced myself to take a deep breath as I looked around. And I found carnage.

Cars had crashed all around us.

Pen's body lay mangled and broken a few meters away from me.

Aarin was fighting with two great big winged guys as three others all bared down on my frightened friends and me.

Their wings were different to the ones I'd seen so far. Where Drake's were pure white and Cadriel's were pitch black, these were broken and burned. The white looked dirty with soot and the edges of the feathers were charred, some still with an orange glow as though they were perpetually burning.

"Serenity!" Aarin yelled.

"We are here for the bride," one of the guys said to us as they closed in.

The girls all bunched up behind me, but Harmony stood by side.

"I thought you were supposed to keep all this hush hush," she accused. "Where are your protocols?"

The guy was tall and wide, bigger even than Cadriel or Drake. He wore nothing but cloth pants, his feet and torso bare. His bruised and broken wings pounded the air behind him, sending another gust of air to batter us.

"The Morningstar's actions have suspended all...*protocols*," he said menacingly. "Hand over the bride and the rest of you may live."

"No." Harmony tried to stand in front of me, but I wouldn't let her.

Aarin was losing his fight and, even with him, we didn't stand a chance against five of them. I couldn't focus on the fact that he and his opponents were denting cars and breaking stobie poles like they weren't made out of solid concrete as they fought. I couldn't do anything about the fact that people had to scramble out of the way of their epic battle. I was powerless against the damage they were wreaking on Adelaide's Central Business District. I could only focus on one thing at a time.

"Did Azazel send you?" I asked the guy in front of us, reminding myself I was Lucifer's daughter-in-law and I was a strong-arsed bitch.

The spokesman looked me over, his eyes pausing for a moment on my sash. It was the one Harmony and Tilly had forced me to wear. The one that read 'Bride to Be'. His lack of direct answer told me all I needed to know. They were Fallen and they were here to kill me.

"Take her," he commanded to the others and two stepped forward.

My mind raced as I tried to think of something, anything, that might get us out of there. Around us, people were gawking and calling out things. Explosions went off as the angels battled on. Then Aarin was finally subdued, going down under the weight of the two Fallen.

I swallowed hard. "Fine," I said as I stepped forward.

Harmony and Tilly grabbed at my arm, but I slid out of their grasp.

"Kill me then. But let them live."

The Fallen chuckled, but there was no humour in it. "It is not you we plan to kill, human."

"Then what do you want her for?" Tilly asked, her voice soft and wavering.

"Bait. Killing the Nephilim's wife would be meaningless. But he would do anything for her."

"Raziel," one of the others said to him. "We have drawn enough attention. We should go."

The spokesman Fallen, Raziel, nodded. He stepped up to me and ripped the sash from my body. He passed it back to one of his lackies. "Send it." Then he wound one strong arm behind my back and I felt the familiar bunching of muscles that told me he was about to take flight.

"Wren!" Harmony and Tilly yelled as Raziel surged upwards.

"Get Lucifer!" I called.

I closed my eyes against the air streaming past them and turned into Raziel to try to protect them.

His body was hard and chiselled like he'd been cut from marble and brought to life. There was none of the warmth of Drake's. Raziel was as cold outside as he was inside.

I kept my eyes closed until I felt solid ground under my feet again and opened them to find I was being tied to a big metal pole, my arms behind my back.

Wind whipped my hair and clothes. Unsurprising when I realised I was on a roof and there were no other buildings taller than us. All around me was open sky, dark and chill even for the middle of summer. Although, maybe the chill had more to do with the Fallen than it did the weird weather patterns we'd been having.

The Fallen stood around me, looking out across the sky and I knew what they were waiting for. They were waiting for the tell-tale sign of wings on the wind that signalled Drake was coming to save me. I was both desperate to see him and terrified what would happen when he turned up.

As it turned out, when they finally arrived, the latter was the more pressing concern, just not for the reason I'd been expecting.

16

Drake

But our laughter was short-lived as a sash wafted down from the ceiling. We leant over to it and saw it read 'Bride to be' on it.

"That's weird," Thane hiccoughed.

Something else floated down and landed over it.

"Fuck. That's not good," Cadriel muttered.

"Is that…?" I asked, not wanting to believe it.

Cadriel sucked in a sharp breath. "I don't want to say I told you so, Morningstar–"

"Then don't."

"Drake," Thane started, "They wouldn't. Would they?"

"Those fucking bastards!" I snapped, standing up so quickly the table was upended.

The sash slid across the floor, as did the burned feather that had landed on it.

"Samyeza!" I called and he looked around. "Up for going after some Fallen wankers?"

He pushed the stripper out of his lap and stood up, a grim grin growing on his face. "Just tell me where, Nephilim."

"Uh, slight problem…" Thane said.

I looked at him and the fact he was a little blurry around the edges as he swayed a little on his feet reminded me what that problem was.

"We are so fucked," Cadriel sniggered.

I shook my head. "Nah, we can still take 'em," I snorted.

Cadriel's pitch black wings sprouted out of sync, unseen to the human eye. "This is going to be interesting."

Samyeza and I unfolded our wings. Samyeza picked up the Fallen feather from the floor and rubbed it between his fingers to get a feel for where the Fallen had taken my wife.

"Three drunks against who knows how many?" I asked.

"We've got this," Samyeza said.

"Wait!" Thane laughed, holding up his hand. "Wait! I'm coming, too."

"Really?" Cadriel asked.

Thane nodded and made a motion that looked like he was miming having a wank. We all snorted a laugh.

"Nope. Wait…" He tried again and, this time, his Scythe appeared in his hand. He nodded at us with pride. One tap of the Scythe on the floor and he was clad in his robes. His voice now whispering rustle, he said, "Right. Got it."

"Let's kill some Fallen bastards and get my wife back, boys."

Using our amazing ability to tell Earth's physics to fuck right off, we followed Samyeza's excellent tracking abilities to a roof of a tall building not too far away from where we'd been.

As the winged members of our party alighted on solid ground, Thane appeared out of the shadows. Although, it was slightly less organised as it could have been as Thane bumped into me and I avoided his Scythe just barely.

"My bad," he said.

"Drake!" I heard Wren call and looked around.

She was standing, tied to a metal pole. I took a few steps toward her, but Samyeza put his hand on my arm.

"The Fallen," he said. He might have been drunk, but he was on high alert.

I nodded and looked around for the wanky bastards.

Five silhouettes materialised in front of us. They were all tall, masculine, and had wings rippling behind them. Even with them half-shadowed, I could see their wings were jagged – courtesy of the wrath of Grandad who, stories said, made them endure Hellfire licking at their wings for eternal punishment in return for their betrayal.

"Oh, shit!" Thane breathed as the Fallen walked forward and their faces left the shadows.

I echoed his statement as the one in the middle was immediately recognisable.

"Raziel." Cadriel stepped forward and I felt the hate burning between them.

I put a hand out to stop him going any further. "Give me my wife," I told the Fallen.

"Your *wife* can leave when you are dead," Raziel said.

"You can suck my dick," Cadriel said as he walked towards him.

This time, there was no stopping him. As he and Raziel stalked towards each other, weapons materialised in their hands. Raziel with his blade tipped staff and Cadriel's standard great axe twirled in his hand before the two enemies clashed with enough force to make the sky rumble as though a thunder storm were threatening.

I looked to Samyeza and shrugged.

"Death to the Fallen arseholes," he said before he went for it.

"Well, best do as I'm told then," Thane said from next to me.

We shared a fist bump and into the fray we went.

It was five hulking Fallen warriors against a drunken motley crew. Still, Grigori never shied away from a fight and they had trained me well; if anything, the truth made us bolder. Thane, unused to fighting, did his best.

Samyeza took on two of the Fallen, leaving one each for the rest of us. He was the biggest and he was the strongest of us. For now.

It was nothing like sparring with Cadriel where we played at a fight to the death. This was actually a fight to the death. The only difference was that one of us couldn't die and the rest were nigh immortal.

The fighting boomed and crashed as we moved at lightning speeds. I knew well the idea that some people thought that a thunder storm was the gods fighting. And this was the first time I really appreciated that.

I ducked a wayward Fallen wing and crashed into Thane and Cadriel. Cadriel's bag of truth burst, showering us with about twenty hits of the glittering powder all at once. And the good shit was always fast-acting.

Cadriel sniggered. "Fuck."

I sniggered. "Fuck."

Thane giggled. "Oops."

Not that we had time for more reminiscing over our sudden misfortune because each of us were grabbed by a Fallen and pulled back into the fray.

"Dude!" Cadriel called as he tripped over his own feet. "Drake! Dude!"

"Yeah?" I replied as I bumped into Samyeza who righted me again.

"Oh, yeah!" Thane cried as he swung his mighty scythe. "Tell her!" It was a fucking good thing that he was the only being totally immune to his scythe because he conked himself in the back of the head with it.

"Tell me what?" Wren yelled.

"Yeah," I agreed. "Tell her what?"

"Our discovery."

"Oh, yeah! Hey, Wren!" I yelled as I ducked under Raziel's swing. "Wren!"

"What?" she snapped.

"I love you!"

"That's great, babe. But do you think maybe now isn't the time?"

"Excuse me?" I pulled up short then grimaced as I felt Raziel's blade slide between my ribs. I turned to him with a glare. "Do you think you could give me a moment here, dude?"

"Drake!" Wren yelled. "Why don't you just focus on not dying!"

"Pfft," Thane raspberried loudly as he dodged the another Fallen's blade. "It's not his time. Yet."

"What do you mean yet?" I asked as Raziel said, "It is if I have anything to do with it."

"Not if I've got anything to do with it," Cadriel snarled as their blades clashed and their faces almost touched.

"First, I'll kill the Nephilim, then I'm coming for you, Grigori."

"I've been looking forward to wiping your worthless arse from existence a good long while, Fallen," Cadriel sneered.

"Promises. Promises," Raziel purred.

One of the other Fallen knocked me to the ground and I struggled to get out from under him as he pressed his blade towards my heart. Everything heightened to a terrifying clarity in my head and my wounds were both distracting and grounding.

I felt the pressure building in my body. Between the bloodlust and my growing concern I couldn't get Wren out of the perilous situation I'd put her in, my emotions were threatening to explode. I could feel the heat in my veins.

"It's over now bitches!" Thane cried excitedly, in no way the impartial being he was supposed to be.

"Supernova!" Cadriel whooped.

It was dangerous to not try to stop it with Wren around, but if it was the only thing that could get us out of there then I had no choice. That's why they'd taken her, in the hopes it would stop me. Nothing was going to stop me protecting my wife.

With a grunt, I placed my hand on the Fallen's chest. With a blast of hellfire, I sent him crashing into a wall behind him. I spread my wings and used them to push me standing. I saw Cadriel and Raziel were the closest. Raziel who had taken my wife.

Heedless of their fight, I grabbed Raziel and pulled him around to face me as my other fist drew back. Using all the power I possessed, my fist slammed towards him.

A flash of light exploded around us and I couldn't move. Raziel's face was millimetres from my fist, but I was frozen. But so was he. I looked around as best I could and saw so was Cadriel, Samyeza and the other Fallen. Thane was turning about and trying to work out what was happening. I wasn't the only one confused and annoyed.

"What is this?" Raziel snarled.

"I leave you alone for one night," I heard and I sighed.

"Morningstar," Raziel sneered.

"Raze, pleasure to see you," my father said, his tone implying the exact opposite of his words.

"Release me, Morningstar."

"Hm…" Dad pretended to think about it as he stopped beside us. "No. See, I like havoc on Earth as much as the next devil. But you messed with my family, Fallen. And I will not stand for that. Mm. No."

"When the Almighty hears–"

"*My father* can go frolic among his singing clouds and tiny winged babies for all I care," Dad said venomously. "But do not insult either of our intelligences by suggesting he gives a flying fuck about what happens outside his perfect little afterlife bubble."

"Michael will–"

"Not tell him anything. Same as the last few millennia. It's just us now, Fallen. And Azazel will be lucky to get you back in a matchbox."

"Just get Wren safe and leave him to me," I said, my eyes locking with Raziel's.

Never mind his feud with Cadriel. I was going to put the fucker down. He dared touch my wife? I was going to take one of his wings and shove it up the lips he never kissed with.

Dad turned to Wren. "Ah, yes. Serenity, dear. How are we doing?"

She gave him a weak smile from her pole. "I've been better."

Dad nodded. "Of course you have." He turned back to me and Raziel. "If I release everyone, will we all promise to behave? Everyone is already terrified of the apocalypse. Angels battling in the streets? Kidnapping brides? PR nightmare, boys. And I do not look forward to sorting it all out. So." He clapped his hands. "We're going to forget all this happened and if I so much as catch a whiff of barbequed angel, I will lay waste to the lot of you." He looked between us expectantly. "Say nothing if we all agree."

I opened my mouth, but no sound came out. I turned my glare on my father. He waggled his eyebrows at me.

"Wonderful," he said.

With a wave of his hand, Wren was free. She stumbled a little as she rubbed her wrists. With another wave, Cadriel, Samyeza and I were free. I let go of Raziel and immediately went to Wren.

"Are you okay?" she asked, looking me over.

I nodded. "I love you."

"Not the time, son," my father warned.

I wrapped Wren up in my arms and held her tightly.

"Such fun, fellas," Cadriel said, tipping an invisible hat to Raziel who growled.

"When I next see you, Grigori, pray to your heathen gods that your babysitter is close at hand."

"How many times?" my father muttered. "I am not a heathen."

Dad clicked his fingers and we were back in his mansion, the Fallen presumably back on the rooftop still. The first thing he did was go to the bar. I still held Wren close to me, her face buried in my chest. But, for the moment, my eyes were on my old man. For a guy who had almost infinite power over the cosmos, he looked quite shaken.

Wren

I almost felt high. Adrenalin surged through my body and I couldn't decide if I was about to burst into hysterical giggles or hysterical tears.

Not even facing off against Cerberus in guard-dog mode had been as terrifying as being on that rooftop while winged creatures – and Thane – battled each other like something out of a film.

I finally pulled myself out of Drake's embrace and took a deep breath as I looked him over. His wounds were healing as I looked at them and I couldn't shake the memory of him under that Fallen.

That must have been the supernova I kept hearing about.

Something like fire had swirled around him, making him shine from the inside out. His eyes had glowed brighter than the sun and I'd felt pressure in the air as though something huge was coming. My heart had been in my throat as I'd been almost certain that he was going to die. That, or my fragile human body would be destroyed in his attempt to save me.

It was obviously a testament to how mad I'd gone that I was more angry at myself for being so fragile as I was that Drake had put me in a position for that fragility to really be a problem.

There was something slightly unsteady about him, a glassiness in his eyes and a vague smile at his lips, as he looked down at me.

"I didn't know Nephilim could get drunk," I said softly.

He snorted. "Truth."

I blinked. "What?"

"Veritas gave Cadriel a bag of pure truth and it exploded in our faces. Literally. And save me, the good stuff's potent."

I had no idea what any of that really meant, but I was guessing they'd taken some kind of super drug.

"I love you," he said again and my heart skipped.

He'd never said it that directly before that night and now it seemed he couldn't stop saying it.

"I love you, too," I told him.

"I also love you, man," Thane said.

I looked around Drake and saw he was sitting slumped on the couch. He was in his robes, his hood down, with his head leaning back and his eyes closed. He cradled his Scythe like he'd forgotten he was holding it.

"If you'd be so kind as to put that away, Thanatos," Lucifer said as he stepped over Thane's long legs.

Thane cracked an eye and looked at his Scythe. "Oh, yeah." He seemed to flick his wrist and it just disappeared.

Lucifer started saying something, but Drake took my hand and started dragging me upstairs.

"What?" I asked him.

He just shook his head as he pulled me to the bedroom.

"I'm really not sure about this, Drake," I told him.

"Why?" he asked as he closed the door behind us.

"Because I'm sure you're too drunk to be making appropriate decisions right now."

He grinned. "If you're a bad decision, then I want to make it every day for the rest of time."

He swept me up into his arms and I put mine around his neck.

"I could probably be on board with this," I said.

"Probably?"

"Maybe."

"Well you'd better decide quickly because we're getting married next week."

I nodded. "We are."

"And I, for one, am actually looking forward to it."

"You are?"

He nodded. "I am. A lot of the planning was stressful, I'm not going to lie–"

"I thought you couldn't?"

"The first and foremost reason why I'm not going to."
His smile was unnecessarily charming. "But it's going to
make you happy and I want to make you happy."

"You're drunk is what you are."

He nodded quickly. "Very."

"You said it was truth?"

"I did. It is."

"How do…take truth?"

"Much, I'm told, like cocaine."

"What?"

He shrugged. "You snort it, mix it in a drink, inject it.
Cadriel was seeing this nymph once–"

"Like dating?"

Drake snorted. "Grandad, no. They were just fucking
semi-regularly. Anyway, she tried baking it into biscuits for
him once."

"How did that go?"

"He told her how he actually wanted to be banging her
sister."

"Oh," I couldn't help but laugh. "So, not the way she'd
hoped."

"No. Truth doesn't just make you answer things with the
truth, but makes you compelled to speak it."

"Like a conscience?"

He shook his head. "Not really for the person on truth, but the ripple effects are similar."

"So, if I asked you what your plans were for the rest of the night?"

He grinned cheekily. "I would quite like to take you to bed and spend all night making love to you."

I nodded. "I could be on board with this."

He laughed and carried me over to the bed. "I am so pleased."

We undressed quickly and fell into the bed together. He laced our fingers together as our legs entwined.

"What?" he asked with a rough laugh.

I looked at him. "What, what?"

"That thought just now. Barely formed."

I felt a slight warmth in my cheeks, but looked him in the eye. "I thought you were trying not to read my mind."

He frowned and wrinkled his nose adorably. "No. It wasn't that."

I smiled. "Not… I meant in general."

"Oh. Right. Sorry. I will try harder."

"Thank you."

He nuzzled me close as his hand trailed meanderingly around my body. "To answer your question, yes," he said.

My cheeks heated again. "I didn't ask a question."

"Well, you asked a couple of questions. And the answer to both is yes."

"All right, smarty pants. What was the question?"

I'd barely caught the beginning of it in my mind before I pushed it away. I wasn't sure if I wanted to ask it at all, let alone get the answer. But he seemed to think he knew.

"Yes, it's possible for us to have children," his voice caressed me lightly. "Yes, I could definitely be persuaded to have them with you."

"And if you weren't on truth?"

He rolled on top of me, his leg going between mine and tempting them to part. "Then I probably would have just answered the first one."

I wrapped myself around him and he slid into me effortlessly. It was soft, it was slow, it was lazy. After all, we had all the time in the world.

18

Drake

I wasn't wary about much on Earth. But I was wary about Wren's Gran.

She was this tiny little thing, all big glasses and skin like a sultana. Sometimes, she acted as deaf and blind as a post, and others she heard you whispering from a mile away.

"You know," Wren said as we followed Gran up the escalator. "I'll kind of miss growing old."

A pang of guilt flooded me, but I hid it pretty well. "And why is that?"

Wren sighed happily as we stepped off the escalator and even my long legs were having trouble keeping up with Gran. "Because she gets to say whatever she likes and gets a free pass," Wren explained.

"Such as I'll die of old age before you get to the crockery section?" Gran asked, turning to us with a knowing look in her eye.

Wren nodded. "Just like that."

"If it makes you feel any better, you can say whatever you like anyway. You're Lucifer's daughter-in-law, I assure you they'll all give you a free pass."

Wren smiled as she hugged my arm. "Actually, that does make me feel better," she said.

"And Kyle?" came the all-too recognisable voice.

I looked down and saw the devilbum peeking around a display case.

"What are you doing here?" I asked him.

"Kyle wanted to help."

"Come on then, Kyle," Gran cooed, as though it was perfectly normal for a devilbum to go to the department store with you.

I looked back to Samyeza who was, for once, doing a pretty good job of keeping nothing but a watchful distance. Honestly, you'd think after millennia of being called Watchers, they would have been better at it. Not that I minded quite so much anymore.

"Kyle stay?" he begged.

I nodded. "All right. But you're not to touch anything. Understand?"

Kyle nodded. "Understand."

Kyle hurried between us and Gran as she made a beeline for the crockery. We were finally getting around to choosing a dinner set with her. We had a week before the wedding, but Gran had insisted we take the time out. Not that we really had all that much to do by then. It was mostly either already done, or had to be done closer to the time.

"You want something classic," Gran was saying and I noticed Kyle taking avid note. "But also, something bold. You don't want it to age but, when you're my age, you want people to know you've had it a long while. That's the sign of a good dinner set."

"How about something like this," I asked, holding up a plate.

Gran whacked me with her walking stick. "Don't touch them! We at least want to get them home before you start dropping them."

"She remembers who I am right?" I whispered to Wren.

"She's deaf and blind, not senile," Gran chided and Wren snorted.

"This one?" Kyle asked, holding up a plate he'd found.

"Oh, sweetie," Gran cooed. "You be careful with that. Let Gran hold that for you."

I looked at Wren pointedly, but she just shrugged and tried to subdue a smile.

We wandered the crockery section and I felt more than useless. You needed to torture a bunch of souls for eternity, I'm your guy. You needed to battle Fallen angels or oversee Faustian Fridays, I could handle it. But pick out a dinner set, particularly when I wasn't allowed to touch anything, I am not your guy.

I was, though, Wren's guy, so I stuck it out as best I could. And honestly, by the end of it, I actually quite liked Gran.

She gave me a whack a fair few times, mostly for picking the wrong kind of china.

"That's not maroon, that's fuchsia," she'd say, practically rolling her eyes. "What are you going to do with tomatoes?"

Or, "Yellow? Sure. If you never want anything gold in your house."

There was also, "You're going to put gold with the silver cutlery, are you?"

And when I'd suggested plain white? I'd managed not to get hit or told off – I'd even been told it was a sensible idea – but that's when I discovered just how many different kinds of plain white dinner sets there are. And yes, they are all vastly different. Or so I was told.

"No," Wren said kindly. "See how this one as a little ridge, and that one doesn't?"

When she pointed it out like that, I could see it and it made sense. Maybe.

"Which one do you like better?" Gran asked.

I looked between what, realistically, looked the same to me.

"The ridge…" I said slowly, convinced that anything I said at that point would be wrong.

"Smooth one," Kyle said and I looked at the little traitor.

"The smooth one is better." Gran nodded.

"I'm going to regret this," I said resignedly. "But why?"

"Because the light doesn't catch, casting a shadow which then looks like dirt."

I picked up one of the plates with a ridge and looked it over. She wasn't wrong.

"Of course, it does."

I vaguely heard Gran say something about shapes, but I was distracted by movement to my right. I quickly scanned the floor and saw Samyeza over by the casserole dishes. As soon as he saw my face, he started looking around as well.

With a couple of hand signals and looks, we determined it was probably Fallen. But it wasn't anyone I knew. Presumably Samyeza didn't know them either.

Almost too late, I saw him barrel his way towards me, wings twirled around him as he span through the air. Moving faster than the human eye could detect, I carefully picked Gran up and moved her out of the way.

The Fallen went sprawling in the aisle and Samyeza was on him.

Meanwhile, Gran still puttered about as though she was oblivious.

Wren was a little less so.

"What just happened?"

I shrugged. "With what?"

"Where's Samyeza?"

"Busy."

She looked me over. "Do we need to go?"

"Don't show 'em they've won," Gran said, brandishing her cane. "Fight them with your last breath. Stand tall and proud. Show them whose boss."

"Appreciate the sentiment, Gran. But not sure that works on Fallen angels."

"Pfft," she scoffed. "It'll work on anyone. You just ask your grandfather."

"He's dead," Wren said.

Gran nodded. "He is. And I can bet he," she pointed her cane at me, "can find him."

Wren looked at me and I shrugged.

"I don't… I don't know who he is, so…"

"A lazy gadabout with a gift of the gab," Gran said knowingly. "Mark my words, Shaw men are a heck of a lot more trouble than they're worth." She looked to Wren and amended. "Except your father. It missed him somehow."

She moved away and Wren looked at me for a moment. "When we get back, can we look for my grandfather?" she asked.

I nodded. "After that glowing review, I can't wait to meet him."

And there was nothing sarcastic about that remark.

19

Wren

We were two days out from the wedding and I was finally not the only one in panic mode. Tilly and Harmony were both on board with the panicking as we put the finishing touches on the table centrepieces for the reception.

Samyeza had interrogated the Fallen from the department store and it was apparently just him working alone as he happened upon us by accident. It seemed the general consensus was to leave Drake alone until Azazel had his strength back after Drake's attack.

But that was currently rather low down on my priorities.

Mum and Truman were running through the millions of lists to see what else needed to be done. With everything we ticked off, I felt slightly better and my stress levels dropped somewhat.

Ignacio was still holed up in the shed on his secret project that no one was allowed near. It had, at least, given

Dad a decent excuse not to do any gardening for the last few weeks.

And Kyle, upon hearing about glue guns, had decided he must help. He was currently staring up at Harmony as she showed him how to glue the diamantes onto the jars.

"Squeeze it slowly," she said. "And just put a little bit on. Not too much."

"Or it will get lost," he said with a nod. If there was one thing about Kyle, he enjoyed learning about new things. Until he got bored.

Drake had told me Kyle was young, the equivalent of a three or four-year-old human, and, from the little I knew about kids, I believed it. At least, though, his bored was quiet. Usually. He'd simply find something else to do. So quiet, in fact, that no one noticed what he was entertaining himself with until he was covered from horn to hoof in diamantes.

"Oh…" Harmony said slowly.

"I didn't even know we'd bought that many diamantes," Tilly said, looking around the table for our stash of them.

"Shiny," Kyle said with a big, wide smile.

"Very shiny," I agreed. "Who needs a disco ball when we've got you?"

"Oh, my," Mum said as she came back into the room.

"Indeed, ma'am," Truman agreed.

"I think someone needs a bath and bed," Mum said.

Kyle hopped off his seat and started making for the stairs. "Kyle bath, but Kyle keep shiny."

"I will help him, ma'am," Truman bowed and hurried out after Kyle.

"How are we doing on the stash?" Harmony asked.

Tilly counted up the centrepieces. "We're two short."

"I've found the last packet of diamantes," I said, holding them up.

"Do you think Kyle's going to turn up to your wedding looking like a giant, walking disco ball?" Tilly asked.

I shook my head. "He'll probably pick them off tomorrow when the glue starts itching his skin."

"I think he looked sweet," Harmony said. "At least he had a good time and he's a happy little guy."

"Unlike Ignacio, you mean," Tilly added.

"Yes, unlike–"

"Boss-lady?" came the guttural grunts of Ignacio himself.

Both Tilly and Harmony jumped guiltily.

I looked at him. "Oh, hey. How's your super-secret project going?"

"Finished."

I tried feigning disinterest so as not to put him off. "Cool. Truman's got Kyle in bath if you want to help?"

Ignacio shook his head. He didn't move from his spot in the door, nor did he say anything else.

"Did you…did you want something, buddy?" I asked.

He gave a single nod. "Present."

I schooled my expression so he didn't know how excited I was.

"Okay. Want me to come and see it now?"

He nodded and shuffled off towards the back door.

"Can…we come too?" Mum asked.

Ignacio didn't say no, so the others followed me out. Ignacio pulled open the shed door and waved his arm inside.

I'll be honest, we entered cautiously. Mostly because it would be just like Ignacio to have been playing with explosives and think they were an awesome present. And they would be…for him.

The light was on and in the middle of the shed floor were three wooden panels. As I got closer, I saw that they were engraved.

"Did you do these, Ignacio?" I asked him.

He nodded and pointed at them.

I knelt down and saw the first one was something I recognised. Stylised but recognisable. It was me 'facing off' against Grace at the gate to Hell. Flames flickered around us. She looked far more menacing and I looked far more heroic than I remembered,

The second one was me standing up to Cerberus. Again, he looked much more fearsome and I looked pretty good myself.

The third one was me rescuing Kyle from the souls in the river.

"I distinctly remember that being the other way around," I said as I pointed at it.

Ignacio shrugged.

"They're amazing. Thank you."

"Wedding gift," was all he'd say on the matter.

But, when I caught his eye, I opened my arms and he gave me a super quick hug before muttering and shuffling off to busy himself about packing up the tools he'd been using.

I looked at the panels again and shared a smile with my mum. "Aren't they great?"

"They're amazing. No wonder he's been locked away in here for so long."

I caught Ignacio looking at me like he wasn't sure if I really liked them or was just being polite. I gave him my warmest smile. "I really love them. Thank you very much."

There was a hint of a smile on his face as he turned away and all I heard him say was, "Family."

We exclaimed over them for a little bit longer, then went inside to put the kettle on and finish the centrepieces. By the time we got in and back to work, Kyle was upstairs curled up at the end of my bed and Truman was double checking the lists.

"Did you know what Ignacio was doing out there?" I asked him.

He looked at me over the paper in his claws. "He wanted it to be a surprise, ma'am."

"And it was. They're wonderful. I feel like they're not quite factually correct, but I appreciate the sentiment."

"If we all bothered too much about fact," Truman said with a wry smirk, "then we would have no remarkable stories."

"I don't know, I think our little journey was pretty remarkable even without the added muscle and stunning jawline."

Truman's smile softened. "Perhaps it is less about how you see yourself, ma'am, and more about how he sees you."

"What do you mean?"

"I mean, that you are an exceptional young woman who has reminded our master there's still some humanity in him. And some of us appreciate that."

"I wouldn't have thought hellspawn would appreciate that."

Truman inclined his head. "Yes and no. Master Drake will not be less than he was by remembering his humanity. You strengthen him, ma'am. And he will need all his strength in the coming years."

"Why?" I asked. "What do you know?"

Truman shrugged. "Very little of use or interest, I assure you, ma'am. Merely that Nephilim numbers dwindle to record lows and this puts him in danger. If he is ever to truly be the last, then even the gates of Hell and Cerberus will not stop the Fallen from trying to complete their mission."

"This is a big thing, then?"

"It may not eventuate to a big thing. But it is not a small thing."

"Truman…" I started. "Can I ask you something?"

"Of course, ma'am."

"If Drake and I were to have children – a child – would they be in danger as well?"

"Less angel means less easily traced, so perhaps not. No. Why ma'am?"

I shook my head. "Just curious as to how it all works."

"I couldn't rightly say, ma'am. To date, no known half Nephilim's have ever existed."

Half Nephilim. Any child of ours would be half Nephilim.

"Because they can't?" I asked, even knowing that Drake couldn't lie.

"There is no reason why they can't. Were I a betting soul, I'd say it was the fact that most don't live long enough for children of their own. Not every soul is lucky enough to be spirited away to Hell where his father can keep an eye on him for millennia."

I nodded. "I see."

Something wasn't quite adding up. I wasn't sure what it was. Only that I felt like I needed more information. It would have to wait, though, because in two days' time I was getting married. And, so long as Azazel and his Fallen didn't crash it, then I could happily wait.

20

Drake

Nothing about the lead up to the wedding had been normal so I certainly didn't expect the actual wedding itself to be normal. But what I didn't expect was the cavalcade set up to proceed me to the chapel.

It was like some sort of New Orleans street parade. Naturally my father had decided my wedding needed to be made public spectacle. I would have been more pissed off if I didn't know (hope) that was the only way he could show his pride and excitement. So, I totally – begrudgingly – let him have it. What did I care as long as I met Wren at the alter at the end of it?

Dad marched proudly at the head of everything in his impeccable suit and a staff in his hand like a proper parade leader. Behind him were a group of succubi, somehow managing to look classy and slutty at the same time as they danced and marched down the road.

Next came the Princes of Hell – these were the ones with a capital 'p'. Mammon. Asmodeus. Leviathan. Baal. Belphagor. All were dressed in tuxedos and rode motorbikes, great big hulking beasts of machines decorated with literal hellfire. Their full head helmets were wreathed in flames flickering in the shape of a crown.

At a stately pace behind the Princes came the Horsemen. Conquest astride her pure white charger. War on his stallion red as blood. Famine atop her black as emptiness mount. And Death upon his pale horse, in full robes with his scythe in hand.

Behind them, Cadriel and I had motorbikes of our own. Big black things that roared no matter how slow we were going. Dad had made us go without helmets, but it would take a holy amount of damage to hurt us. Ignacio hung onto the back of mine and, when I turned to check on him, his tongue was lolling out of his mouth happily.

Thane looked back at me from his pale horse, his robes turning slowly. It wasn't his fault he'd been created to be the spectre haunting the nightmares of the living. So yeah, he exuded fear. The eerie, ethereal floating of his robes and the gaping black hole where his face should have been were enough even to send a small chill up my spine. But he was a good guy.

Music came from somewhere and I didn't really care where from. It was impossible for me to even begin to speak to Ignacio, let alone Cadriel, over the roar of the bikes so we rode in otherwise silence until we pulled up in front of the church. People lined the roads to watch us pass and I would have felt more antsy and uncomfortable under their gazes had I been concerned that people would remember it when it was all over.

I was quite sure that, once the celestials and supernaturals had faded back into obscurity that humans would start calling hoax. Those who'd personally witnessed events would start to doubt they'd seen them. Videos of my father's shenanigans would be put down as some elaborate publicity stunt. Much like the murderous clown craze I'd heard about, the circus would suddenly be over and people would start to forget it ever happened.

Dad was waiting for me at the front doors of the church and I climbed off the bike. Ignacio leaped off and stalked inside ahead of us.

"Ready, son?" Dad asked as Cadriel stepped up beside me.

Thane dissolved his robes and was left standing in a tuxedo that matched Cadriel's and mine. I looked to my – well I guess calling them anything less than friends after everything would be a disservice – friends. Cadriel gave me a single nod and Thane gave me a thumbs up.

I nodded to Dad. "As ready as I'll ever be."

Dad clapped me on the shoulder as he started dragging me into the church. "That's my boy. No better way to go into a marriage than kicking, screaming and desperate for the door."

I sighed.

"I think you'll find humans think the opposite," Cadriel said as he looked around.

"Cadriel!" the priest called.

"Lachlan," Cadriel said as he walked over to meet him.

Strangely, he was a personal friend of my best man. It seemed weird to think of Cadriel as having friends – myself included – and even weirder when it was a priest. But it wasn't like that. Father Lachlan wasn't one of those priests headed straight for my father's version of the afterlife. Rather, he and Cadriel had become friendly when they realised they could have quite educational and deep debates about the whole religion thing.

On some level, I didn't know whether Father Lachlan actually, completely believed that Cadriel was a Grigori. But that wasn't relevant to me or the fact that the priest had seemed happy enough to facilitate the wedding of the son of a guy claiming to be the devil.

Guests were starting to arrive and the age-old debate of bride's or groom's side became pretty easily settled quite quickly. Mine wasn't the one with the impeccably dressed humans.

Esther was there in the front pew next to where my father would be sitting if he wasn't busy flitting around and greeting people. And I meant that quite literally. He was zipping around the church faster than the human eye could catch, stopping to introduce himself to someone or say hello. At times he even peeled away from himself and was in duplicate between the pews.

Larry and his a capella group floated in a row, being eyed off warily by a young human on the other side of the church. There were demons of various species. Grigori were in attendance as though they weren't little more than the hired muscle. Truman and Ignacio were trying to keep a rowdy bunch of devilbums under control while Kyle got a little overexcited by everything as the light glinted off his few remaining diamantes. Even a couple of my half-brothers were sitting behind their mother.

It was a full house in more ways than one. I could just imagine what our wedding photos were going to look like compared to the usual ones.

"The humans are taking your side of the church better than I expected," Thane said.

I nodded. "I feel like my father had something to do with that."

"Makes sense. Last thing we need is a military standoff."

"He's been waltzing around Earth the last two months, totally not hiding who he is. It'd be hard for them not to believe it by now."

"You would be surprised what the human mind is capable of believing – or not believing – when it wants to," he said quietly.

"Seats, please," Father Lachlan called. "The bride is here."

I looked up quickly and saw Sam walk in with Wren's Gran and take their seats in the front. Kyle ran down the aisle, then suddenly stopped and looked between them like he didn't know which side to sit on. Sam beckoned him over and he ran to sit with her. Gran patted his head like it was totally normal to bring your devilbum to church with you.

Once everyone was sitting down, the opening bars to the wedding march flowed out from the organ, sounding a little more haunting than the typical. The doors opened as though by their own accord and I looked to my father, who shrugged innocently. The gathered guests all stood and my eyes were pinned on the door, waiting for that first glimpse of Wren.

Harmony walked in first, looking beautiful in her off-white silk gown and holding a bouquet of lilies. Tilly came behind her, in another off-white silk gown but of a slightly different cut, one that suited her perfectly. Both of them were halfway down the aisle and I was getting impatient when I finally saw her.

And then my world stood still.

My heart calmed.

My mind emptied.

I could die happy just looking at her.

Her dress was beautiful in its simplicity. It was cream lace and tulle, with a sweetheart neckline and draping off-the-shoulder sleeves. But nothing had ever seemed so perfect. Her hair was up, but whips brushed her shoulders and around her face. And her smile blew me away.

I'd never had cause to doubt I wanted this – her. Eternity didn't seem like such a long time if I had her by my side. But I couldn't lie and say that I'd loved the white wedding side of things. All the planning and interference had driven me near mad.

The sight of Wren gliding towards me down the aisle, though?

I'd marry her everyday if she wanted.

Nothing was too much effort for the reward.

Brian walked her too me, sparing her a kiss on the cheek and me a telling nod before he lay her hand in mine and took his seat.

Father Lachlan welcomed everyone to our wedding, but my eyes were glued to Wren's.

"Hi," I said quietly.

"Hi." She bit her lip and her eyes fucking shone as she looked at me.

"You look beautiful," I told her.

"You're not so bad yourself."

I tried to suppress at least the force of my smile, but it was impossible to hide it altogether. Especially when she was smiling at me like she'd never been happier. It was a sentiment I understood.

Father Lachlan got the ceremony underway.

"If any man under God objects to this union, may you speak now or forever hold your peace," was a bit we'd put in as a bit of a joke. Considering we were already married under their laws, we had no expectation that anyone would want or be able to object to what was a simple ceremony.

So, when the doors crashed open, the entire chapel was surprised.

Wren and I turned. There was a great hulking figure, surrounded in blinding light, standing in the doors of the chapel.

"Who is that?" she asked, her hand squeezing mine.

You ever wonder where my dad got his dramatic flair? You're looking at him.

Had I ever seen him before? No. Did any of the millions of iconographies from around the world get his visage right? Probably not. Was he wearing a robe of any kind? Did he have a long white beard? Were there any signs of clouds or lightning? No. No. And no.

But I'm the son of the devil. A role that comes with perks. Perks I've fully embraced and work for me effortlessly.

So, I knew exactly who had just crashed my wedding.

Cadriel stepped forward and I put my arm in front of him surreptitiously.

I sighed. "That would be my grandfather."

Dad stood up quickly. "What are you doing here?" he asked indignantly. And he thought I had Daddy issues…

Grandad walked forwards, some of the blinding light dissipating to a more eye-friendly glow. "I came to see if a Nephilim was actually marrying a human, son."

I couldn't tell from his tone if that was a good thing or a bad thing. As much as I knew about him, he could easily have Azazel and his bunch of pussies standing at the ready outside.

Wren

Half the chapel had stood up like they would personally fight their Creator to ensure this wedding happened. The other half were whispering among themselves. I didn't blame them.

Actual God was at my wedding. He was even in a tux. His close-cropped beard and slicked back hair were both grey. The term 'silver fox' crossed my mind unbidden and I hoped Drake wasn't in there. I snuck a look at Harmony and Tilly and knew I wasn't the only one.

"And what exactly were you planning to do if it was?" Lucifer asked, crossing his arm petulantly.

God spread his arms out wide and looked around with a wide smile. "It would hardly be a family affair without the patriarch of the family. Don't you agree?"

Lucifer frowned. He was losing some of his usual extravagant flair and gaining more of the sort of vibe you'd expect from the Lord of Hell. His whole posture changed.

He wasn't the put out, sullen man-child anymore. He was the Devil. Strong. Powerful. Commanding. Angry. Slightly insane.

"I wasn't aware it was convenient for you to play at patriarch just now."

"And miss my grandson's wedding?" God's tone was jovial enough, there was even a smile at his lips, but his eyes were hard as he stared at his son.

There was a very real showdown between Heaven and Hell going on and I didn't know what the fall out was going to be.

"Because now you care about him?"

God smirked. "Well, it's not every day your grandchild marries someone sane *and* willing, is it?" He was quite clearly making a joke, but it flopped spectacularly. That laughter he was quite clearly waiting for wasn't coming.

You could have heard a cricket chirping in there, it was so quiet. A tumbleweed rolled across the front of the church and I snuck a look at a very innocent-looking Lucifer.

"Drake," God said warmly as he came up to us. The church doors closed by themselves as he did.

My husband cleared his throat. "Grandad. You… You came."

God nodded as he looked around. "Of course, I did."

"Why now?" Drake's voice was accusing.

"It's been a good long while since a human walked right into Hell. And for my grandson, no less. I figured at least one of you must be incredibly special."

He sniffed and nodded. "Wren's not like most humans."

"No, I see that."

There was pregnant pause, in which there was silence in the church but for the rustling of people shifting uncomfortably and a rogue cough.

"I..." God started. "I have a gift for you. For your wedding."

Drake's eyes narrowed. "A gift?"

God nodded. He pointed towards the doors and they opened to reveal a blinding light. Through it walked a shadow. As they got closer, she solidified. In the dark recesses of my mind, I recognised her. And it was just as Drake's reaction confirmed my suspicions that I remembered her.

"Mum?" Drake asked, taking a step towards her then stopping as though he was afraid she'd disappear again.

"Just for the day, mind."

Drake looked at God then back at his mum like he couldn't quite believe it.

"Go on," God encouraged gently. "Go and say hello."

Drake looked at him once more, then jogged to his mother, who met him halfway down the aisle. The threw their arms around each other and mine weren't the only eyes threatening tears.

I looked at God and smiled. "Thank you."

He smiled back. "After everything, it was the least I could do."

"The least," Lucifer scoffed. "The least would have been leaving us to it. Who even invited you?"

"When you marry in my house, it's kind of a given. Don't you think?"

Lucifer huffed and dropped into his seat. He kept looking over his shoulder at Drake and his mum. I wanted very badly to know what was going through the devil's head just then. After all, he was the reason Drake's mum was dead. But I wondered if it went deeper than that. Had she just caught his eye for a night? Or did he have feelings for her once?

Drake talked quietly to his mum and God gave a single nod at the sight.

"Shall we... Shall we continue?" Father Lachlan asked hesitantly.

God nodded. "No. Please. By all means."

Drake said something to his mum, then got her settled next to Lucifer in the front row and hurried over to me again. The smile on his face was one of pure happiness.

The priest looked at the two of us. "Shall we?"

I looked at Drake. "Ready?" he asked me.

I was ready. I was more ready than I'd realised. Now we were here, I had no qualms about marrying Drake. Quite aside from the fact we were already technically married, I had no reservations about making it official by human laws and traditions, in front of our friends and family. Even if they were quite a varied bunch.

I knew who I was now. I knew who I wanted to be. I knew what I wanted to do.

"Do you Drake Morningstar take Serenity Shaw to be your lawfully wedded wife under the eyes of…" The priest paused and slid a glance at God. "God?"

"I do," Drake said.

"And do you Serenity Shaw take Drake Morningstar to be your wedded husband under the eyes of…" Another pause. "God?"

"I do," I said, smiling at Drake.

"Then by the power vested in me, I hereby pronounce you man and wife." A huge cheer rang out through the church as he said, "You may now kiss the bride."

Feeling like I was bubbling over with happiness as much as my husband, I stepped closer to him and kissed him. For us, it was chaste. For a church in front of our families, it maybe involved a bit too much tongue.

The organ started up. Drake took my hand and led me down the aisle. People threw rose petals over us as others cheered again. When we got outside, Drake picked me up and spun me around. I laughed and he kissed me deeply. When he pulled away, he was smiling.

"Your mum's here," I reminded him.

He put me down and looked around at the guests flowing out of the church. "Come and meet her."

People showered us with congratulations as we passed them until we got to his mum and he stopped short. I could feel the nervous hesitation in him and couldn't remember ever seeing him unsure of himself. Not like this.

"Mum," he said as she reached out to him. He took her hand and looked at me. "This is Wren. My wife."

She looked at me and I finally saw she had a watery quality to her, like she wasn't quite so solid after all. She also seemed to emanate a faint glow.

"You've certainly grown up a lot since I last saw you," she said to me.

"It's been a while, Miss…" I'd suddenly forgotten what Drake's last name used to be.

But his mum smiled. "Call me Maya, dear. We're family."

I nodded, just realising how surreal it was to have your husband's dead mother's ghost at your wedding. But then, it wasn't all that surreal for me. It felt totally normal. Then Thane wandered by with a nod and I realised that ghosts were quite possibly the least weird thing about my wedding day.

But I loved it – I loved Drake – and I wouldn't have changed anything for the world.

The reception was a huge affair. Lucifer had spared no expense – monetary or mystical. It was in the middle of a field under a canopy of fairy lights and giant marquees. There was wooden flooring to protect against those guests who chose to wear heels. There were festively decorated tables, bedecked with flowers and golden confetti. The waiters bustled about, attending to your simplest whim. And everyone was dancing or eating or laughing.

It was perfect in every sense of the word.

Honestly, I probably would have been happy with a family trip to the local Maccas. It was the people as much as the atmosphere that meant I ended up with sore cheeks from smiling so much.

Larry's a capella group serenaded the party for a while, and Lucifer even got up with his fiddle once or twice. There were, unsurprisingly, lots of songs about devils and angels, and these were the ones that got the biggest reaction from everyone. Unlike the dinner party Lucifer had hosted for me in Hell, anyone dancing at our reception was dancing of their own accord.

God hung around for a while, blending in with the rest of the guests. At one point, Lucifer sidled up to him and I saw them have what looked like a bit of an awkward conversation. It was interesting to see Lucifer almost looking like he wanted someone's approval for once.

At midnight, Maya came up to say goodbye.

"I'm so proud of you, Drake," she told him. "It means the world to see you found your happiness."

"You can't stay any longer?"

She shook her head, resigned to her fate. "I've had one more day with you I never thought to have. Let's just be glad we get to say goodbye this time."

"I hate him for taking you from me," Drake said.

Maya smiled sadly. "Your father is who he is. Don't blame him for things you don't understand."

Drake frowned. "I don't–"

"Time to go!" Lucifer said loudly as he came up to us. "It's been lovely Maya."

For a split second, he seemed totally sincere. And the way she looked at him. Understanding passed between them and I was left with the singular feeling that there was much more to the story than Drake knew.

Maya hugged her son and me one last time.

"I'll see you again," Drake promised her.

She nodded. "If anyone can, it's you."

God held his hand out to her and they walked off into the night.

I was sure I heard Lucifer sniff but, when I looked at him, he was gone.

Drake seemed a little melancholy for a bit after his mum and grandfather left. But it didn't take him too long for him to shake it off. It might have helped that I made him dance with me and our bodies were rubbing up against each other almost inappropriately for public.

"Are there anymore mums I need to meet?" I asked him.

He laughed. "No. No more mums. And, Seph and Mum are the only two who matter."

"Poor Esther," I chuckled.

Drake shrugged. "I honestly don't think she has feelings, so I'm not sure she cares." As he looked down at me, his eyes went from blue to red. "I love you, Wren."

"And I love you."

He kissed me as we danced until Harmony jostled us with a laugh as she danced with Thane.

It had been the perfect wedding. Everyone who mattered to us – and then some – had shared it with us. Drake was my husband for something like the third time over. I was his wife. Soon we'd go back to Hell and start a real life together, the literal kind of forever.

I honestly didn't think that anything could have made my new reality more perfect.

...continue the story in Book 3.

Damned if I don't

You can check out the playlist for this series on Spotify. Just click or scan the QR code.

Thank you so much for reading this story! Word of mouth is super valuable to authors. So, if you have a few moments to rate/review Wren and Drake's story – or, even just pass it on to a friend – I would be really appreciative.

Have you looked for my books in store, or at your local or school library and can't find them? Just let your friendly staff member or librarian know that they can order copies directly from LightningSource/Ingram.

If you want to keep up to date with my new releases, rambles and writing progress, sign up to my newsletter at https://landing.mailerlite.com/webforms/landing/y1n6q2.

Follow me:

Thanks

To all the usual suspects.
That's all I've got this time.

My Books

Scarlett's list is just starting out, but you can find where to buy all my books in print and eBook at my website; www.elizabethstevens.com.au/.

About the Author

Scarlett Knox is the Paranormal Darker/Bully Romance penname of bestselling author Elizabeth Stevens. Scarlett is the name to read if you want darker/bully romance in the Mature YA/NA crossover space with paranormal elements. Think high school, college, and academy. Add in superpowers, vampires and werewolves, angels and demons, and more. Scarlett brings my usual wit, banter, and repartee in good old enemies-to-lovers showdowns between alpha males and the sassy heroines strong enough to kick them to their knees.

Writer. Reader. Perpetual student. Nerd.

Born in New Zealand to a Brit and an Australian, I am a writer with a passion for all things storytelling. I love reading, writing, TV and movies, gaming, and spending time with family and friends. I am an avid fan of British comedy, superheroes, and SuperWhoLock. I have too many favourite books, but I fell in love with reading after Isobelle Carmody's *Obernewtyn*. I am obsessed with all things mythological – my current focus being old-style Irish faeries. I live in Adelaide (South Australia) with my long-suffering husband, delirious dog, mad cat, two chickens, and a lazy turtle.

Contact me:

Email: scarlettknox@elizabethstevens.com.au
Website: www.elizabethstevens.com.au/scarlet-knox
Twitter: www.twitter.com/writer_iz
Instagram: www.instagram.com/writeriz
Facebook: https://www.facebook.com/elizabethstevens88/

www.ingramcontent.com/pod-product-compliance
Lightning Source LLC
Chambersburg PA
CBHW011201190726
48286CB00009B/2870